LATITUDE

Writing from
the Philippines and Scotland

LATITUDE
Writing from
the Philippines and Scotland

Angelo R. Lacuesta **and** Toni Davidson

EDITORS

ANVIL

Manila

Published and exclusively distributed by
ANVIL PUBLISHING INC.
8007-B Pioneer St., Bgy. Kapitolyo, Pasig City 1603 Philippines
Sales & Marketing: 637-3621; 637-5141; 747-1624; marketing@anvilpublishing.com
Fax: 637-6048
Website: www.anvilpublishing.com

Cover design by Michael Manalo
Interior design by Ani V. Habúlan

ISBN 971-27-1725-9

Printed in the Philippines

Editors' Notes

WRITING CAN BE A NATIONAL CONCERN; it can reflect, deplore and subvert the traits of the culture from which it emerges. Such national concern can infuse the writing with idiosyncratic dialect and unique perspectives while the themes can explore personal and political situations that draw on both modern and historical experience. But writing is also international, not just in terms of translation but in terms of voice, methodology and, above all, soul. The soul of the writer, the heart of the words and their meaning are truly *sans frontiere*.

Latitude seeks to reinforce that international sense of writing which allows both for the uniqueness of the writers in their own environment and the ability for it to travel, not just translate, to a completely different place. Completely different? Perhaps not. The overall 'youthful' feel to the collection reflects new ideas on familiar themes but these familiar themes are given new twists and the howl of anger and lust and desire for things to be different is given new voice.

When I visited the Philippines for the British Council in 2002, I was struck by the passion and energy of the writers I met. I was surprised too, being ignorant of Philippine history, how for many of the writers English was a mother tongue in terms of their writing and yet also how strong the bilingual influence was. I felt, rightly or wrongly, I was around something new and strident; an exciting time as writers debated the use and fusion of the language of their writing voice. There was a vibrancy and enthusiasm to the work and many of the writers who I met are included in this anthology. There was also a seriousness that belied their youthful vigour. There were many things to write about a society and a culture that was by no means perfect and yet contained within the narratives was that all important factor—readability— where prose that chose to subvert, challenge and, on occasion, shock still encouraged the reader to carry on reading and understand that this writing with its many themes and perspectives has value; immediately and in the years to come. In the Philippines, in Scotland and wherever the world sets up a stage.

Toni Davidson
Glasgow, March 2005

THIS BOOK IS THE RESULT OF A FRIENDSHIP. I met Toni Davidson while at the 6th Philippine-British Literary Conference held in Manila in 2002. We struck an easygoing friendship, revived through email and the odd telephone call.

Glasgow is, quite literally, half a world away. In 2003 I visited Scotland on a month-long Hawthornden Fellowship, enduring 14 hours of flying time, 4 hours on a train, 2 hours on a bus and half an hour in a black cab, not including downtime at airports and train stations. Over furtive day trips to Edinburgh and a visit to Glasgow, Scotland further established itself as a world of a different order. At the Center for Culture and Arts in Glasgow, Toni and I spoke about picking up where we had left off on the anthology project we had discussed two years before. In fact, he had taken the initiative then by sending me, as early as 2002, a sheaf of stories that would make up the bulk of the Scottish side of this anthology.

When Toni paid a return visit to the Philippines in April of 2005, it was clear that there was no turning back. He had made good on our literary friendship and galvanized me into taking action.

The Filipino side of this anthology combines new and well-established names, with a good mix of voices and concerns. But there are strong and recurring themes. One subject that appears in the work of young and old writers is the confrontation Filipinos must make—and continuously make— with the West. This confrontation is most evident in the language in which we write: a language that is native to the Scottish culture and of a second nature to many Filipinos.

Pinoys are a well-traveled lot. So are the Scots, it seems, as Toni himself proved on his last visit to our country, going as far as the mountain cities of the North and the islands of the South. These collected stories will further reveal other similarities: that both cultures are proud people, eloquent, artistic and whole. Still, this book represents a first dialogue. I only hope that this exchange will spark other, similarly rich conversations and friendships.

This project would not have been possible without the faith and persistence of my co-editor and of many people whose support and guidance have proven valuable: Gill Westaway, Karina Bolasco, Ani Habúlan and Chin Martelino.

Sarge Lacuesta
Manila, December 2005

Acknowledgments

"Like a Pendulum in Glue" was first published in *Damage Land: New Scottish Gothic Fiction* ed. Alan Bissett (Polygon, 2001)

"We Global Men" was first published in *Penmanship and Other Stories* (Cacho Publishing House, 1995)

Toni Davidson acknowledges support from the Scottish Arts Council towards the publication of this title.

The editors would also like to thank Gill Westaway, director of The British Council, Philippines, for her generous hospitality and encouragement.

Contents

GRAHAM BELL

A Director's Story

WHEN HE DIED the director left no witnesses to the event. This came as no surprise to those who knew him for he had always been essentially a very private man. But in the newspapers and on local television, the unsolved mystery of his death became more famous, perhaps than any of his films had been for a long time. A body in a sealed room always arouses suspicion.

His country was a democracy now but rumours still flew that members of the military junta he had always been a quiet opponent of may have been responsible for the death. For years the civil war had raged and while never overtly supporting the revolutionaries it was clear to those who knew him that he was on their side. His fame had perhaps protected him. In fact, not long after the military coup when the junta had begun seeking out and 'disappearing' its opponents the director had gone into hiding for several years.

At the time his family, wealthy and respected, had disowned him. But of course when the revolutionaries marched triumphantly through the streets of the capital they had welcomed him back with open arms. The people were not so forgiving however and if not actually banished most of them found it easier to emigrate than to stay.

It was many years later when he so mysteriously died and left a will which puzzled many. His films were always involved and cryptic so to those who had known him it seemed only appropriate that his testament should take the form of a conundrum.

The beneficiaries had to gather at his remote country house and were to be presented there with a series of clues in the form of short sequences from his films, clues which would help them discover the answer to his riddle.

For like his films, which infuriated many since they offered no easy solutions, no quick final resolution in the closing frames, it seemed the director's life had been centred around contradiction. In the last few years of his life very few people had seen him and his films seemed to appear from nowhere puzzling audiences more and more while the critics went into raptures over their opacity.

Most of the beneficiaries were unaware of this since they had left the parochial backwater their country had become for them many years before. Only his executor knew the full story.

As they watched the sequences of film it seemed as if the director had somehow managed to piece together fragments from *their own* histories.

And so the band of strangers—for many of them had lost touch in exile— became accomplices determined to solve the problem. For only when they had worked out the meaning of the circumstances around the director's death would the details of the will be made known.

But at times it seemed they would have to watch the entire history of film before solving the mystery. Then at last the day dawned when the final reels were screened. Scandalous! This time they agreed he really had gone too far!

The final reels contained footage of the beneficiaries themselves in scenes they never remembered as having happened to them. At first they couldn't understand how this could have happened until they realised that the images were slightly blurred and in fact looked as though they had been superimposed into different backgrounds. The disjointed soundtrack was even more confusing—it seemed to bear no relation to what was happening onscreen.

Their immediate reaction was outrage and they cursed the executor for helping to dupe them. He insisted he knew as little as they did but was lucky to emerge unscathed from the angry scene.

Then as they began to calm down they realised that this was perhaps the most important piece of the puzzle. And so they reasoned it out—none of them had actually seen any of the directors movies and if these films represented his career he must have been some kind of impostor, duping a gullible nation with work that was no more than badly put together voyeurism.

Even the executor had to ask himself if perhaps they weren't right—at least for the last few years the directors films had seemed a little obtuse and now he came to think of it—when was the last time one had been shown in a cinema? He himself began to doubt the director who had been his friend for years.

It was then he decided to open the penultimate envelope. The directors wishes had to be carried out according to a series of envelopes which could only be opened at the discretion of the executor and he felt the time was now right to open the penultimate one. Its contents seemed to confirm everyone's suspicions but if that was the case—who had their mysterious benefactor been?

For hours they argued with the executor insisting that he open the will immediately but despite his reservations he still believed the man who had been his friend deserved to have his final instructions carried out to the letter. The mystery of the director's death had still not been solved.

They returned to the screening room to watch the films once more and see if they could find the answer there. . .

It was then they realised that the answer lay not in the movies themselves but in the credits. In not one film had the director been credited under his own name instead it seemed he had used a string of pseudonyms. That was no surprise the executor told them since the director had a reputation for that very thing.

But looking closer they noticed that despite the fact that the director used the same cast and crew time and time again, not one of them had worked on all of his films. Except for the sound man.

Finally things began to make sense—the disjointed soundtracks had been edited to go with the stolen footage of themselves—some of the footage even looked as if it had been made while they were at his estate! Somebody must have been filming and editing them—perhaps was doing so at that very moment!

At last the executor agreed that they should discover what was in the only locked room in the house—a room to which only he had the key, with strict instructions not to open the door until the case had been solved.

But circumstances had changed and since the people were getting more and more agitated he agreed they could open the door.

In the control room they found that they had been monitored more or less continuously since their arrival through a series of hidden cameras placed throughout the house. And there in a locked writing desk they finally discovered—

"The last will and testament of...

I believe that in the moments of our greatest lucidity we can sometimes become aware of a presentiment of our own deaths. I don't mean the actual physical death that will probably overcome most of us in a slow decay of the body but a death which is perhaps more real than that. This death is the ideal one and embodies a secret, a secret we are most of us ashamed to impart.

For in those final moments all the pressures of life disappear, we realise that we are ultimately alone in the universe and on the brink of something we may never really "know." For I do not believe it is given to the human mind to understand what comes after death whether that state is simple nonexistence as so many believe, or the fires of hell and a transcendental oneness as the religious would say. And, at last, after years of searching I finally know what my death will be.

It takes place in a smoky room—a library with museum display cases containing remnants... of my collections. There are corals, crystalline minerals, amphibians, a variety of skulls and my pride and joy—a collection of beetles from around the world. There is, the Gestro Stag Beetle from Papua New Guinea, the Gold Beetle from the remotest highland bogs of Scotland, the Speckled Rose Chafer from Sierra Leone and the rare Sagra Beetle from Java the female of which outshine the male in iridescence. Then there is my collections of scarabs—a beetle whose very name in Egyptian described its mystic origin—chaper—the becoming—rare ancient specimens preserved in amber, amulets in greenstone and clay which served to protect the dead.

In the centre of the room is a dais, covered in purple velvet. I enter and lay down on it. My body is smeared in a heady mixture of secretions, pheromones and dung. My silken dressing gown falls to the floor as I lay naked on the dais. A coffin is suspended above it. It has a sealed bottom and the top is glass. Inside are millions of freshly hatched larvae of the Carolina Tiger Beetle, a ravenous predator.

Once I am in position and am mentally prepared for what is to come I pull a cord and at once the whole writhing mass falls upon me. For the few remaining moments before they have stripped away my outer flesh I am in ecstasy as a million coleopteric mouths tickle my body.

When my corpse is discovered there are hardly any signs of the beetles which will have escaped the locked room following a trail laid earlier through a hole in the bookcase to the outside world.

But perhaps one will linger to tantalise the investigators into the cause of my death. It crawls slowly out of the eye socket, glints in the dying candle light and pauses while it digests the contents of my brain… This is my perfect death—what is yours?"

But instead of a will what followed was another riddle. It took the form of a story, many stories, and although they recognised their names amongst the characters there was little direct reference to money or the deeds of the estate.

The beneficiaries were furious, flicking through the pages frantically they sought without success a more straightforward deputation. Then they came across one story that made them pause—it told the story of the director himself and how he made his first film after he had been disowned by his family and had no money of his own. He had lured a group of people to his estate and killed them in a freak accident inheriting their money in the process.

Too late they realised that the executor and all the servants had disappeared. All the doors were locked and the windows bolted. The smell of burning was becoming thicker and thicker. Soon all that was left of the estate was a smouldering ruin.

JOSE Y. DALISAY

We Global Men

THREE BLUE-BLACK FACES STARED BACK AT HIM. It was the color of the print, an oddly cool monochrome postcard that stood out among the more common sepias and hand-tinted photographs bundled in a box marked "The Orient, Etc." He didn't have to look at the printed caption on the upper right-hand corner to know that these were, indeed, "Filipino Children." There were three of them, all girls, caught by the photographer against a fuzzy landscape that may have been grass or newly-harvested rice; bamboo thickets stood out against the sky, far in the sloping horizon. It was a sun-drenched day, with only the strongest features of the girls' faces coming out of the shadows: their pudgy noses and wide mouths, their small eyes squinting against the light, against the curious intrusion of a white man with a large wooden, glass-eyed box into their day. Two of the girls, no more than ten years old, wore the traditional cotton or plant-fiber wide-necked blouses with ballooning sleeves that opened to spindly arms. A dark *tapis* was wrapped around their waists, covering most of their ankle-length skirts. The third girl, about six, wore a polka-dotted shift, a *tapis* or bandanna hooked over her shoulder. Their hair was tied in buns, making their brows seem broader. The leftmost girl held what appeared to be another folded piece of cloth to her mouth to mask her smile. The second girl wore a necklace. All stood barefoot on the side of the muddy road.

He turned the postcard over to see how much it cost. Another man nudged his elbow to reach into a sheaf of cards offering sights of the West Indies; the antique show had opened earlier that morning, and now the place was crowded with dealers and buyers in booths displaying brass sextants, Nazi armbands, animal figurines, leatherbound books, and candleholders, most of which held little appeal for him, except for two heavy metal gadgets which he had thought were tools but which turned out to be boot-scrapers. It was warm in the auditorium, with all those bodies and the heating; outside, a stiff autumn wind was dragging dead leaves to the gutters. He had gone to the show on an afternoon off from business to look for small blue bottles for his wife; he had one of them in the pocket of his parka, about four inches high, rather crudely made but stamped "NOT TO BE TAKEN." It cost him two pounds—about eighty pesos—and he was told that bottle was meant for poison. He felt pleased to be bringing home a token of Scottish pharmacology—not for its own value, but because she would be happy. He would have left at that point, after a quick and final stroll through the exhibits, but then he had seen this postcard and its three unmistakably homegrown faces.

He felt surprised by the sight of flowing script; most of the other cards had nothing on them—had never been sent but had probably been kept by their owners for souvenirs. The blue-black girls had been an early Christmas greeting to a "Miss Brown" of 23 Comely Bank, in Edinburgh, Scotland, from an "Iza Renner" sending his (or her?) "Compliments of the Season." It had been posted from Manila, P.I., 14 November 1910 at 5:30 p.m. The face of William McKinley glowered in vermillion on the four-centavo stamp. The card's price was pencilled in, at L2.50. He thought that a bit much and would have replaced the postcard, but his pocket sagged with loose change jangling against the bottle, so he counted out the money, making sure to rid himself of the heaviest coins. It would make an interesting and ironic souvenir, a conversation piece back home. "I met your grandmothers in Scotland," he would tell someone dryly, "all three of them." He tucked the postcard into the other pocket of his parka, turned up his collar against the cold, and hurried back to his hotel.

He had been in Edinburgh for a week on a training visit for his Canlubang-based company, a manufacturer of agricultural machinery with headquarters in the UK. After Scotland he would fly back to London for a trade show and some shopping, and then to Hong Kong and home. An engineer by training, he felt good to be abroad, to take sugared tea for a change and to bundle himself in woollens, but it was all part of the job, of the dizzying flow of global commerce in the late 20th century. He had been abroad half a dozen times before—to Germany for his graduate studies, to China, India, and the US, among others, not counting the stopovers in places like Bangkok and Seoul.

Their house in Merville Park was stuffed with the ornaments and curios of the middle-class vagabond: teak jewelry boxes crammed with trinkets, silver beersteins and elephants, cloisonne teacups, sandalwood fans, his wife's bottle collection. A woven tapestry from the American Southwest hung on the wall in the dining room. No one visiting the house would have come away without remarking what a fortunate life he led, being away so often. And he made sure to cart home as much as he could of the world, not so much to show off as to reassure himself that anything and everything was, almost literally, within reach.

A month before this trip, he had made the final amortization payment on his four-bedroom bungalow, and a year-old, bluish-gray Nissan Sentra waited in his garage. The two kids went to good schools, and his wife Elaine pulled in her own money as an editor of technical and corporate publications. They had put some of their savings in stocks, and with the recent boom in the market, they looked forward to affording a trip to Disneyland, and to visiting their relatives on the East Coast. He was only in his mid-thirties, and life ahead—barring the kind of major upheaval that meant a messy change in governments and business policy—could only be a pleasant series of promotions, one or two more babies, more travel to some dreamy place like New Zealand or Bali, and retirement to a farm and an orchid garden in Antipolo or Tagaytay, high above the smog of the sprawling city. He didn't believe himself to be that financially secure, not yet—he would put his Christmas bonus, he promised, into a long-term time deposit—but he felt rich with accomplishment and opportunity. If he died in a plane crash, his soul would go to business heaven, with a three-million-peso insurance policy to be paid out to his family. He had every reason to feel satisfied with what he had done.

In Edinburgh, he was billeted at the Clarion, a medium-priced hotel on Palmerston Place, within a stone's throw of the stately granite buildings overlooking Princes Street, the city's prime commercial artery. On the other side of the Gardens stood the towering hulk of Edinburgh Castle, "the most famous of Scottish castles," his hotel guidebook said, "dating back from as early as the Norman period."

The Clarion with its kilted maitre d' wasn't exactly to his liking—he preferred, for some reason, the impersonal efficiency of American hotels—but he appreciated its location and its tidy business center on the third floor, with its humming computers and fax machine. He had taken along his Powerbook, of course, with its 100-plus megabytes of surplus storage, but there was nothing more soothing to him than to know that wherever he was, if his own systems went down, he could dial himself to the office and to Elaine in the living room. He could forgo the bagpipes, even, as far as entertainment was concerned. Culture, to him, meant a gift shop in the lobby and a ceremonial glass of the local brew.

A woman in a store on Princes Street had offered him a kilt—which a Japanese tourist was being fitted for—but he found it ridiculous to even imagine himself wearing a skirt. He had been profoundly more interested in a scale model of Preston's Steam Engine at the Royal Museum. There were better things he might have done with his evenings, spent slouched before the "telly" or hunched over his laptop, but he could save the real fun for London: the plant visits and briefings had been exhausting, and commanded all his professional attention. He had a reputation for uprightness and thoroughness to maintain. The trip to the antique show at Meadowbank Stadium was a necessary detour on Elaine's behalf. He would just as soon have stayed in his room and relaxed with an hour of TV soccer, which he missed from his years in Germany. He had a dinner meeting scheduled with his hosts later that evening; he expected to be served haggis, and was thinking of an excuse to order a porterhouse, served medium-well.

He took the elevator ("the lift," he reminded himself) up to his fifth-floor room, taking the blue bottle out of his pocket, where it was making an unsightly bulge. He put the bottle on the nightstand, undressed, and took a shower. Bach's "Brandenburg Concerto" was playing on the room radio, and he was struck by how close the melody was to a cartoon theme—Popeye, that was it: *para-PAM-pam-pam, pararararam-PAM.* He thought of the short speech he would have to make at dinner, but he was good at these things, and his English, though American-accented, would see him through. Over the past few days he had accustomed himself to the peculiarities of Scots English, with its burrs and distended vowels; the plant supervisors he had dealt with said "sexty" when they meant "sixty," and so forth. They seemed surprised that he could understand them, as much as they could understand him. It was, for many of them, their first encounter with a Filipino who wasn't a maid or a nurse's helper. He imagined that they expected him to speak in some kind of Japanese or Swahili, and he was glad and proud to disappoint them; if they knew German, well, he could speak some of that, too. He felt like an ambassador at large, from "The Orient, Etc."

He shaved, brushed his teeth, slapped cologne on his cheeks, put on a fresh change of underwear, and chose his clothes carefully. He picked out a deep navy blue suit, a white shirt with thin gray stripes, and paused for a minute between a red paisley and a black-and-olive regimental tie, settling on the newness of the paisley, a stopover purchase at the Hong Kong duty-free. The red would go well with his cordovan oxfords. He would look businesslike enough, but warm and friendly. "How do you do?" he said to the mirror, pressing a dimple into the tie. He wondered if an overcoat was called for by the occasion or the temperature, but he would not be walking: a car and driver would come for him in thirty minutes, and he would wait in the lobby. He felt no pressure at all.

He was about to leave the room when he saw his parka where he had thrown it on the couch. It offended his neatness, and he hung it in the closet. He remembered the change remaining in the pocket, and took it out for tips. He felt a stiffness in the garment, and saw the postcard again. He did not know why, but he put it in the inner pocket of his dinner jacket, along with some business cards he had drawn from his Filofax. He stepped out into the hallway and caught the lift, squeezing in behind a smelly American backpacker and an Austrian couple who, he was glad to gather, were arguing about whether or not they had locked the kitchen door at their home in Innsbruck.

He had a sherry—nutty and medium-dry—in the lobby while he waited. He scanned a rumpled copy of *The International Herald Tribune* for news from home, but there was none; another neo-Nazi march had been broken up by the police in southern Germany. He remembered the embroidered swastikas and the foot-long daggers at the antique show. He felt relieved not to be in Germany at that moment—he had gone to school on a scholarship at a university in Marburg—but Germany and its anxieties seemed distant now, when no one could possibly mistake him for a foreigner who would impose himself and his needs on the social security system of another country. Things were very different from where he sat. A capped chauffeur called out his name, and he strode out to the car with the cultivated smartness of someone who had learned to dress from a series on business fashions in *Management Today*.

JUST AS HE HAD EXPECTED, dinner at the Howtowdie, a Georgian basement restaurant on the West End, was an all-Scottish affair, from the soup ("cullen skink: a creamy blend of smoked Finnan haddock, onions and potatoes") to the obligatory haggis ("a Socttish dish made from sheep's or calf's offal, oatmeal, suet and seasonings boiled in a skin made from the animal's stomach"), Loch Etive mussels, and hot goat's cheese on oatmeal toast, washed down with drams of Bowmore Islay single malt whisky, with water on the side. He had decided on the ride to quell his misgivings about the food and play the jolly good fellow, and his sporting stance and his little speech in praise of international economic cooperation had been rewarded with gravelly cheers and further toasts from his hosts—a Mr. Forsyth, a marketing director of the parent company, and a Mr. McTaggart, a technical consultant who had spent some time in Japan.

McTaggart seemed eager to show off his expertise in Asian culture and affairs, and the Filipino obliged him with confirmatory nods as he worked belatedly on his chocolate pudding; it seemed the only familiar flavor in the place. "Nothing we're doing here that they can't do or haven't already done there, I say," McTaggart said. "We're retooling the Leith factory, as you know, with software systems developed by Fujitsu."

"I mightn't go so far as to say that," Forsyth said amiably, refilling his shot glass. "Surely there must be something new and unique here that our friend can take home with him, or we would've wasted his time. The Philippines, aye, now there's a country to be watched... What time does your flight leave, by the by?"

"At 8:40," he said, adding quickly, "in the morning."

"Good, then I'll have the driver come by for you at half-past-seven, will that be all right?"

"Yes, thank you very much." The pudding caught in his throat and he took a sip of water.

"More whisky?" McTaggart said, but before he could answer, McTaggart had poured him another shot. "Pity you haven't seen too much of Edinburgh. It's a lovely city, really, although it must be frightfully different for an Asian, these stone buildings and all—"

"I'm used to the West," he said. "I did my master's in Germany."

"Aye, aye, indeed, I do remember seeing that in your c.v.," McTaggart hastened to apologize. "I haven't met too many Filipinos overseas, actually... Except—oh, well—when I was in Japan, in Osaka—you should have seen them dancing!—" McTaggart stopped abruptly to pat his lips with a napkin. He was a large man with green eyes and curly hair the color of dried coconut husk. It framed his pinkish cheeks in sideburns, and something wet had fallen onto his woollen gray tie.

"I understand." He thought of all the Filipino bargirls who sat on the laps of whisky-swilling businessmen in Osaka. They were "cultural entertainers," as their visas would have noted, and he had patronized many of their shows himself, back home, on nights out with clients. He had seen nothing wrong with that; he could afford them. But now he felt a twinge of shame and anger, as if McTaggart had gone out of his way to insult him.

"We have a subsidiary in Osaka. Gavin here did some splendid work for them," Forsyth explained, forgetting that McTaggart himself had been making the point all evening.

"Yes, of course," he said. He looked at the whisky and decided to drink it all. "Tell me, Mr. McTaggart—"

"Gavin, please—"

"Tell me, Gavin, what did you think of those Filipinos? In Osaka?"

McTaggart shifted in his seat and folded his arms together. He had sensed the injury in the Filipino's tone of voice, which seemed unnecessarily unfriendly. "Well, I—I thought very well of them indeed, I must say… Very pretty lassies, if I may be so candid, and very brave. Very brave. To think they would leave home and suffer winter and—and such other inconveniences—for a job."

Forsyth understood nothing, and asked, "Were they working in the factory, Gavin?"

"They must have been," the Filipino said—to save McTaggart, despite himself. An image flashed in his mind of the Reeperbahn in Hamburg, and of Amsterdam, wide windows full of women, mostly white but in all colors, and he felt an odd, unsatisfying sensation of revenge, of a form of compensation that wasn't what he needed. Wood was singing and popping in a picture-perfect fireplace somewhere in the room; he could hear it in the silence, and yet not feel its heat. McTaggart was looking in its direction, seeking comfort there.

"Well—you have an early flight tomorrow," Forsyth said, raising his finger to the waiter for the check.

The Filipino reached into his pocket for his business cards, but touched the postcard there. He was surprised to remember that he had bought it, and wondered why he had taken it along. Had he imagined, perhaps, that he would slip it into the conversation, to remind his new friends of a time when they saw little of interest in his country but the quaint barefoot girls in their native costume? And look at me, I'm here, a man, a businessman who wears good shoes and speaks the languages of the world. Don't you see?—I'm one of you now, we're all in this together, we global men. But the postcard seemed to burn in his chest, to weigh down his whole body, to draw him back to something he had struggled long and hard to leave. His hand remained protectively beneath his jacket, and soon Forsyth's brow was crinkled in alarm.

"Is—is something wrong? Do you need some medication?"

"No, I—I think I should be going," the Filipino said, praying that Elaine was home.

Lizard Luck

JAKE SCANNED THE ENDLESS ROWS of deliciously tempting bottles and, for a moment, he had to admit a grudging respect for man's ingenuity. For all appeared to hold within them the promise of other worlds. But most of all they held the twisted kiss of comfort, a gleaming half-way house somewhere between the twins of oblivion and pleasure. Tall and short bottles, fat and skinny ones, stood side by side with those that had been chiselled from pure diamonds. And each was stamped with labels as diverse human desires.

Drink me. Suck me.

Hold me. Love me. Lick me.

Trust me.

But Jake's eyes were drawn immediately to a bottle of Chinese liquor on the top shelf, oddly alone amongst its compatriots. It had a grey tattered label with faded blood-red Chinese characters spilling off the sides in an avalanche of bizarre text. It spoke of a monochrome world of iron curtains mixed with a dash of stubborn cold war mentality, shaken, not stirred. Like an ugly duckling the bottle was unattractive and at odds with the sexier Western alcohol that had been so meticulously groomed in the art of seduction.

Having asked the barmaid for a closer look at the bottle, Jake turned it around in shaking hands and was shocked to see a lizard. Perfectly frozen in time and suspended in clear alcohol, the wrinkled grey creature appeared to move of its own free will as the bottle shifted from side to side. For a moment he thought it might even be alive. But the barmaid stepped in. It had been here for years. In fact, even the owner of the bar could not remember buying it. And then Jake noticed she was looking at him strangely.

"You were here last night weren't you?"

Jake looked back into her dark eyes hidden partly by curved spidery eyelashes and shook his head. But she continued.

"You drank from this bottle last night. I remember. It was my shift. You were here by yourself in that corner" and pointed to an empty booth upon which a candle burned slowly as though waiting for Jake's return.

And so the scene seemed to be set. Jake took the bottle over to his table and sat down. Slowly he poured a drink into a small but heavy shot glass. The lizard squirmed, its tail wrapping around the insides of the bottle like an umbilical chord. Almost invisible wisps of something green floated around the lizard. Jake felt pity for it and wondered what story it had to tell.

Holding the glass next to the dancing flame, he threw its contents down his open throat. At first… nothing… then something erupted in his chest and stomach. The heat was intense as an atomic explosion, like a burning sun, like déjà-vu nightmares coming true. Then, just when he could take it no more, his entire body was infused with a floating sense of well-being. Breathing deeply, he recognised the faint whiff of an aroma, both vicious and joyous but so slight it could have been a membrane. An emotion perhaps. Then he was drifting in a warm sea, every inch of his skin tingling. He was being licked by a thousand gentle lovers, their soft tongues reaching inside him. Jake shivered with pleasure. He had come home.

"Did ya like that? Did ya?"

Spinning around for the source of the voice Jake could see nothing. Shifting uneasily on his seat, his hairs stood up on end. Deep inside he felt centuries of evolution rising to the surface and noticed that the skin on his stomach was thicker than that on his back. He knew that one time, long ago, he had crawled on his front from the safety of the sea.

Returning his attention to the bottle, Jake could swear the lizard was grinning at him. Again the insistent voice spoke up.

"Are you looking at me?"

Shit. Shit. It was the lizard! It was talking. Wasn't it? Jake shook his head and stared at the creature, seeing his own face reflected in its dark pupils. Sweating, he lowered his head towards the bottle and whispered very quietly

"You, I'm looking at you."

"I guessed that," spat the creature.

Although lizard in form, there was something human about the way its muscles worked. China, thought Jake, seemed like a long way away as he tried to convince himself that the talking lizard was nothing more than the result of an overactive imagination fuelled by the strange drink. But it was off again.

"No, I'm not from fuckin' China. Do you believe everything you read? Even if your brain denies my existence, look at the hairs standing up on your arms—they know I'm the real thing. More real than Coca-Cola! Your body can't be conned but you need to wake up, Jake. Change comes through the barrel of a gun you know."

Confused, Jake stared at the lizard, noticing the way it moved in short sharp bursts whilst speaking. The lizard was on a roll, pulling no punches.

"Man, I don't know how I came here. I was drugged, spiked, hit on the head or something. Next thing I was awake here inside this bottle. Jesus wept. You lot lock your true natures away. Denial is your calling card. For you are only really yourselves when following instinct, feeding off moments, fucking the future in the ass and the past in the eye."

By now Jake's eyes were out on stalks. He felt like a cowboy riding a horse never looking back at his burnt-out farmhouse and mutilated family. Looking forwards was the only way for Jake. There was no choice. If he had a past, it was gone now.

JAKE KNEW HE HAD A BATTLE ON HIS HANDS. Tied between two frothing horses he was being pulled apart at the seams. One, a dappled grey mare, had the insignia of reason stitched onto its worn brown leather saddle. The other, a magnificent jet-black creature, had instinct emblazoned across its flared nostrils. Caught in the middle, Jake's blood supply had been cut off at the wrists by a course rope that led to the two straining animals. He was standing, legs apart, beneath a sweltering sun, arms stretched as far as they could go without being ripped from their sockets.

❀ ❀ ❀

STILL THE LIZARD CONTINUED.

"You are jealous of us. Look what you do to your pets, parading them around as strange little humans, calling them names, dressing them up and lying to their faces! And before you try to defend yourselves, let me make it clear that I know about humans. I have been here for so long now taking notes and watching your struggle that in your world I would by now be some famous critic of human behaviour. My shelf would be full of cheap trophies and badly engraved awards. But instead what do you do? You ignore me and my skills so I have no choice but to do what I do best."

"And what is that?" enquired Jake, for it was becoming clear that he needed to feed the creature's ego.

"You will see, you will see," replied the lizard, "but first let me introduce myself. My name is Leonard, and there are things I would like to show you, experiments we can run together to prove me right. So what do you say Jake? Are you willing to watch the proceedings unfold? You will not be disappointed. Revolution is always fascinating…"

Jake could only nod. At this a broad smile formed on Leonard's face and he started to rock back and forth, his little black hooded eyes opening and closing like some exotic sleepy plant. Jake then asked if Leonard was the bar's entertainment.

"Is that what you're after?" he scoffed. "Maybe you expect me to dance a little jig!"

Looking up, Jake noticed the bar was getting busy. A group of young office workers were talking workplace politics.

"She just doesn't have a clue, the only thing she is good at is bending over for Richard! I can't believe they actually employed her."

"I don't see the point of a job description if it is going to be ignored."

Jake yawned. But Leonard was getting to him. He looked at the aching chasm between the way things are and the way things should be.

As if reading Jake's mind, Leonard spoke up again.

"You see that woman over there, yes, her. She has a crush on the guy at the far table. There are things she wants to do to him that, if done in public, would lead to a prison sentence! The others here all have similar tales to tell. But more of that later."

Just as Jake was turning around for a better look the door burst open loudly.

"Streakers!" shouted Leonard, his tail spinning around in tiny excited circles.

"Bloody gorgeous, aren't they?"

Once again Jake could only nod. Like Tazmanian Devils caught up in a whirlwind they came, shoving and pushing, laughing and grinning, slipping and holding on for dear life, faces lit up with a luminous glow, red mouths open, tongues pushed out, teeth bared, bodies for all to see, the sheer rush of it all.

And then they were gone, the swinging back door the only sign they had ever been there.

JAKE MUST HAVE BEEN THINKING HARD for he heard Leonard's frustrated voice pipe up again.

"Hey you, forgotten me already?! I'm good aren't I? In fact I should have been a magician... no... an anthropologist but they don't deliver home courses to a bar, do they? I wouldn't even need a grant. I don't have overheads... ha ha... I don't have any dependents. I'm what you might call flexible. A real modern guy. But I'm not exactly mobile, am I? And let me tell you something— I still know how to party. And our females—they could teach you a trick or two. There are things they can do with their tails that you haven't even dreamed of!"

Jake liked Leonard but he was beginning to annoy him. He did not blame him for his bitterness. Being trapped Leonard had no choice but to live his life vicariously, through the flickering screen of the bar's television set, the jumbled up sentences of the dislocated drinkers and the catchy tunes from the old jukebox. The rest of us, thought Jake, could walk away. But then he wondered whether it was as simple as that. Where would he go—to another bar?

Looking at the lizard, Jake had missed the tolling of the bell. He was being kicked out.

"Yes, it is time to leave now," mumbled Leonard, "there are laws you know."

Whilst carefully returning Leonard to the barmaid's slim hands, Jake caught a glimpse of somebody oddly familiar in a far corner. A shadowy figure wearing long black lace gloves and a white bonnet sat hunched over a drink like a scientist examining the world through a microscope.

"You have to start at the beginning you know," mocked Leonard as Jake stared at... an ancestor. Peering closer he saw a furrowed forehead, the lines chiselled deep into dark leathery skin and a mass of thick black wiry hair protruding through the bottom of crisp white cuffs. Carrying the weight of the world upon strong but vulnerable shoulders was a monkey, her eyes huge, hazel and almost bashful. A love song, as soft as a tear, played gently on the juke-box.

Back amongst the bottles it was impossible to even catch Leonard's eye. But Jake knew he was watching, planning and up to his old tricks.

This is an excerpt from Mark Waddell's first novel *Lizard Luck*.

¡Que lastima!
Espero que tu se mejore

BART HAD BEEN COMING TO THE ISLAND FOR SO LONG that he knew all the tricycle drivers unto the third generation. To test his memory, he tried to recall all those whom he had known in the Biblical sense. Why, if they had been female, he might even have sired one of these young men now driving motorcycles with sidecars that had been passed on from their fathers, or painfully bought through years of labor and lonely exile in the deserts of Saudi Arabia. The possibility filled him with virile pleasure and an almost teary-eyed magnanimity. He grew nostalgic at the mixed odors of brine, sweat and gasoline, and forthwith prepared a large tip. The familiar sight of the young driver's raised muscular haunches, his bare, tanned legs, the heels bleached by salt, pumping at the gas pedal to start the motor, filled him with tenderness. He wished though that their perpetually grinning driver would stop calling him *Tio'y*, the local term for uncle. True, Bart knew his father, and had known him too in the distant past, in the Biblical sense as well. He had lent him the money to buy him his motorcycle years ago, which made him practically family, he supposed, a benefactor at least. Bart tried to make a joke out of it.

"Don't respect me so much," he gently chided the young man identified as Noli by the fluorescent green fringed nameplate swinging from the canopy of his tricycle. Noli was only a boy really but a very well-built boy. Bart squeezed his brawny shoulder. He must just be out of high school, if he had even gone past the sixth grade. "Bart will do fine."

"Yes, Sir Bart," Noli persisted, not even looking him in the face.

"Or 'Papa.' He hasn't been knighted yet, so don't call him sir. Papa Bart would be very nice," Melo wryly suggested.

There were so many tourists at this time of the year. *Tourist Galis,* Melo called them. He sucked in his gut, unpleasantly aware of his toad-like torso and shrunken, hirsute calves, beetle-like, swimming in his loose Birkenstock clogs. No one looked at him though, which was both a relief and a cause for resentment. It was not pleasant to find that one was growing invisible with age. He missed those days when he and Bart would enter a disco and he would find himself surrounded by eager schoolboys and marine engineers. His dance card was always full then. The memory rankled and left a bitter taste.

If it hadn't been Manolet Alba's youngest daughter Michelle's sixteenth birthday, and the scheduled outing of the *Iloilo Succulents and Orchids Society*, he would have begged off. He had no desire to encounter surreal displays of teats laid out on the white sand: a mammary landscape of innocuous pinks, as pale as sow bellies, or elongated brown zucchinis with distended areolas as large and dark as filled espresso cups. . . flaccid, deflated sacs that would not have been out of place in a Salvador Dali painting. The most upsetting, though, were the glistening golden domes, catching and absorbing the sun's ultraviolet rays with the even efficiency of their suprahuman symmetry. Their perfection immediately gave away the surgeon's craft. The natives were so used to the half-naked foreigners, and only smiled indulgently when other Filipinos alluded to this disgrace darkly. The aesthetics did not matter. As far as they were concerned, it was just an innocuous little quirk that one could easily get used to.

Melo was amazed at how down-to-earth and pragmatic the Filipino *masa* could be. There was that first time as a callow youth, that he had tarried with one of the tricycle drivers in a *kubo* farther up the beach. The driver (who didn't even know how to kiss) had said, "Please wait, Sir. I have to take a shit." Then did just that, right before Melo's horrified yet fascinated gaze, in a corner of the *kubo* where the flooring had given way and scrawny pigs, dogs and chickens foraged and rooted below. Melo had vowed then that he would never eat any pig or chicken grown and bred on that island. Immediately after, without even washing and with just the most perfunctory swipe with an old newspaper, the driver had presented his posterior to Melo who was so over-whelmed by what he had just witnessed that he had to decline. But he had paid him just the same, out of noblesse oblige. It was a class thing, like washing one's hands, or the use of toilet paper for that matter. They had a different set of sensibilities altogether.

Some though, Bart and he had taught how to kiss, as well as to perform other, less familiar but pleasurable acts that had gladdened these country bumpkins. They were unlikely culture heroes: a pair of provincial Prometheuses bestowing the hygienic uses of the enema and the esoteric lore of the *Gay Man's Kama Sutra* into the humdrum existences of these deprived rustics and enriching their lives in ways that went beyond material considerations.

At Villa Allisandra, which Manolet Alba had named after his older daughter who was away at UCLA, Michelle, the birthday girl, was dreamily poised on the verandah over-looking the beach. She held a gauze wrap aloft behind her shoulders and enjoyed its fluttering and billowing, like magnificent fairy wings. She was Aphrodite risen from the waves, and for now, she was content to be delighted by the way that the ocean breezes fluttered the gaudy print of fuschia and hibiscus blooms about her narrow shoulders. She was waiting for the boy she loved to arrive and hoped that he would see her, standing there in the sunlight, amidst the artfully clustered palms, with her hair blowing behind her. He did not know that she loved him because he was her cousin, and she was not supposed to feel that way. He suddenly came up and hugged her from behind. She cried out at the cool weight of his body pressed against hers, then giggled. He was speaking to her in schoolbook Spanish with the most exaggerated accent.

"¡Feliz cumpleanos! ¿Que tal? You don't look well. Have you been ill? ¡Que lastima! Espero que tu se mejore..."

Don liked playing pretend and saying the most outrageous things. Once at the mall, he tried to pass himself off as a Russian exchange student (the only phrase he knew was "Peche mu?" which meant "But why?") She had to be the stereotypical Japanese tourist that time, and discreetly follow a few paces behind him with a camera. She also had to keep her eyes downcast, smile shyly, and say "Hai!" as she waved in tiny flutters and covered her mouth daintily each time she giggled: "Hi! Hi!" They laughed a lot when they were together, which would have been a good sign for any other couple. Except that they couldn't be a couple because they were cousins. Even as an accident of birth, it had tragic repercussions and caused Michelle to feel quite profound and preternaturally melancholy at times. From the dining room, Michelle's mother Cheloy Alba called her to put more sun block on." Mrs. Alba was well-versed in the art of self preservation and used 15 different skin care products on her person each day.

"Buon giorno, principessa!" Don blew kisses at his aunt through the doorway. "Ah, Tita Cheloy looks so happy. She must have just had great sex." Michelle blushed and pinched him playfully on the arm to make him shut up—not that she really wanted him to… She would rather talk to him than to any of her *barkada*. They thought he was gross. She thought they were boring, but never said so, because she was not ready to be a social outcast at this point in her life. Bart and Melo came in and there were shrieks of greeting and air kisses all around, from Cheloy and her friends.

"Those two also. I'm sure they just had sex," Don observed. "Probably had to pay for it too. But cheap—they must get a discount since they're regulars."

"Richard Gere and the gerbils!" Michelle burst out, wanting to show that she was knowledgeable as well. "Wasn't that cruel? Those poor little creatures must have died in there."

"You know some day, I am going to invent robotic gerbils that disintegrate inside the human colon—acting as a dual purpose of fiber-based laxative and hemorrhoid zapper at the same time. I'll make a fortune."

Michelle noticed a raft full of teenage boys adrift close by. She raised the halter top of her purple lycra bikini, to cup her breasts in more tightly. She was convinced that the boys on the raft could not take their eyes off her. Actually, they were too stoned to care. Michelle's friends, mostly from school, and her female cousins, lounged about desultorily, and frowned at Don.

"Hello, chicks!" he greeted them, because he knew it annoyed them. He annoyed them further by offering to rub sun tan lotion on their backs. They ignored him diligently, and went on smoking and drinking beer straight from the can. Valerie Lu, who was Chinese and not even from Michelle's section, whined that you could see her varicose veins through her pale skin. Actually it was just one bulging twisted green vein as large as a peso coin, behind her left knee. She wore a large towel wrapped around her waist like a sarong. She vowed that she would not remove it until she was close enough to the water to run into the waves. Her swiftly moving legs would make that single blight on what she considered to be her otherwise perfect self, a blur too faint for anyone else to discern. But everyone else at the beach house knew about this vein because Valerie never failed to point it out. She considered it an obscene sign, like the miniscule face of an alien twin homunculus she had absorbed in her mother's womb.

Michelle didn't even want to invite Valeria Lu in the first place. She thought her neurotic, stupid and tiresome, but her father made her. Valerie's father, Edison Chiong Lu, owned a piece of property that Alba Realty was very interested in.

"Why, you have very nice legs, Valerie darling," Cheloy Alba assured her. "I don't think you even have to wax them or shave."

"Eeh-yeuough!" Valerie shrieked in disgust and offended the other women playing mahjongg by the verandah, who had to wax and shave, not only their legs, but also their bikini lines. Privately, they attributed her bad manners to her being Chinese and knowingly sighed about all that money wasted on those who could never overcome the handicaps of their race. They pitied Cheloy and Michelle Alba for having to associate with Valerie simply to get into Edison Lu's good graces. But then the real estate prices were down and so one had to do things that were not entirely to one's liking.

"Hey, Val—I can see your nipples and your suit's not even wet,' said Don. Valerie screamed and ran inside to change.

CARITAS DUMONGON ARRIVED AFTER LUNCH with a middle-aged American in tow. Bart and Melo expertly studied his face, fascinating and repellent in its stark plainness.

"Like a cross between George C. Scott and Woody Harrelson," Bart whispered to Melo. "You know, the *Natural Born Killers* actor, the spokesman for legalized marijuana use."

"*Ka-lain gid sa imo…* Not good, not good," Melo shook his head sadly, but inwardly he felt a thrill of secret attraction. It was so easy to picture most Asian men in drag, but there was nothing soft or pretty about this Caucasian face, which was all hard lines and angles. He was also losing his hair and didn't bother to hide it. Caritas's friend seemed to have no feminine aspect, and in a sea of sexual ambiguity, it was a refreshing novelty. The stranger stared back at Melo and Bart. His friendly but unwavering blue-eyed gaze was intense and disconcerting, as though he were memorizing their features. Bart simpered and wandered into the kitchen to compose himself. Noli, the tricycle driver, was there. His mother was a maid at the beach house. He was helping out, hauling in bags of ice cubes and filling the coolers of soda and beer.

"So helpful, and so cute," Bart thought. He caught his eye, and Noli smiled prettily, flashing dimples, then modestly averted his gaze with a downward sweep of his impossibly long lashes. Bart caught his breath and involuntarily clutched at the kitchen counter. He felt like a bar of warm sugar was melting in his chest and spreading to his limbs, sweet though ephemeral. The unspoiled ones were really the best. They flourished like free-range chickens, untainted by nitrates, additives, artificial food coloring, and the other contaminants of over-commercialization and conspicuous consumption. Just like free-range chicken, their meat was so much tastier.

Meanwhile, Melo was making conversation with Philip, Caritas's date. He was an architect and had met Caritas at a street party in Manila some months ago. There was the usual drill about whether Philip liked the Philippines since this was his first visit.

"When I learned he was coming to Boracay, I advised him to watch out for the transvestites," Caritas said.

Philip laughed. "Best travel tip I got. They should put that one in the guidebooks. How to distinguish the Filipino transvestites from the genuine GROs."

When Philip went off to pee, Melo nudged Caritas. "Darling, he looks like a cowboy. Does he ride good? He has such small feet. What is he—a size eight only, I think?" Melo was an expert on shoe size. As a student at the De La Salle, he used to cruise along Roxas Boulevard, picking up Navy recruits and asking them what size their feet were.

"That is no indication whatsoever," Caritas said. "But he is real macho. Super. I took him to this naturopathic healer in Malate for his back. The healer guy took his pulse and read his aura then told him that his male energy was so high, even his feminine side was a tomboy. So now I tease him that unlike the rest of us with an inner child, what he has is an inner tomboy."

The appearance of Caritas with a *Kano* who looked like she had picked him up on the beach, livened up an otherwise dull afternoon for Cheloy Alba and the other matrons. They were gratified that Caritas never learned. They knew most Americans were HIV-positive. He probably had herpes or crabs. But then one could not expect anything better of Caritas Dumongon. She had been found when she was only three years old, on one of the sugarcane railway cars at the Celeste Aida Sugar Central. Her name was Lolita then, and her mother had run away to Manila to become a dancer, leaving her behind. It was learned that the father had long abandoned them as he had always doubted that Lolita was even his child.

The farmhand who had found little Lolita immediately brought her to the spinster Locsin sisters, the owners of the Celeste Aida. The old ladies were nonplussed and frantically discussed whether to bring the child to the Department of Social Welfare first, or to the Asilo de San Vicente de Paul straightaway. The farmhand said that if they were going to institutionalize the child, then he would take her himself and try to raise her as best he could in a loving family, even though he was a poor man with seven children of his own. Menggay, the youngest and most tenderhearted of the Locsin sisters, burst into tears at this lowly farmhand's nobility and generosity, considering that the wages the Locsins paid him, kept him mired in certain poverty. She persuaded her three older sisters that it must be Divine Providence that had left this poor child at their mercy and they could do no less than take this veritable orphan into their home.

In the hushed and embalmed atmosphere of the Locsin house, the child had alarmingly shown her true nature from the very start. Every time she heard a disco beat, Lolita would immediately begin to bump, sway and grind in a manner that would have been quite provocative in someone ten years older. The household servants were delighted and amused at her talent and encouraged her, greatly dismaying Miss Menggay and the older Locsin sisters. All the servants were forbidden to play disco music in the child's presence or to call her Lolita, which the Locsin sisters decided was an unseemly name, carrying all sorts of evil Nabokovian allusions. And so Lolita was hastily re-christened Caritas Ludovina (the latter after the Locsin girls' own late mother). This second baptism was actually an exorcism of the demons of her past. The Locsin sisters called her Ludy and she slept with a maid in Miss Menggay's room. Miss Menggay was prone to nightmares and the maid was actually there for her.

Sometime during her high school years, Ludy decided that she wanted everyone to know what she actually was: an object of the Locsin sisters' charity and a way to upgrade their passage to heaven. She changed her name to just Caritas, and dropped the Locsin for Dumongon, her biological father's name. She also began running away.

"My friends are all wondering where I picked you up, and whether we're screwing each other as a regular thing," Caritas said to Philip.

"Tell them you're getting me by the hour but that I'm very reasonable," he said. "I'm not even in it for the money, just the experience."

"No one would believe that I'd pay good money for you!"

"Oh, now you hurt my feelings. Go ahead. Pick on the white guy. He can take it."

A paunchy, balding Caucasian with a Filipina who looked about fourteen but was probably twenty-three strolled by.

"Look at that! What you say that could be me ten years from now?" Philip asked.

"More like five," said Caritas. "And he has more hair than you."

Philip ruefully touched his bare scalp. "I'm gonna shave off what's left on the sides, babe, then I'm gonna look really cool. You'll see. Probably get an earring, maybe two."

"Don't worry about the hair, Philip. You actually look quite virile without it."

"Yeah, just like those wooden penis ashtrays at the souvenir shop. And that wooden dude in a barrel. Those are just what my flat needs. Some tasteful souvenirs from the Philippines."

Manolet Alba and the popular plastic surgeon Dr. Sergio came outside to watch Michelle and her friends playing with the jet ski. Dr. Sergio had done Cheloy and most of the other ladies there, so they all had the same sculpted, tip-tilted noses. He winked at Philip and declared, "I see you have HIV-AIDS."

"Excuse me?"

"Hair Is Vanishing. *Anit* Is Definitely Showing." Dr. Sergio laughed raucously, then frowned as the jet ski sputtered and the water from its drain arced erratically. "Hey, look at that kid—*mahina... Bata pa, baldado na!* He's so young and his urine stream is not even erect." Manolet and Dr. Sergio waded out, yelling at the kids that they'd show them how to run the jet ski properly.

"You know, my urine stream is always erect," Philip said.

"Do you realize that since we've met, all we've talked about is God and sex?"

"And that's how it should be."

Dusk was falling. The tide had crept away. The young people built a bonfire on the shore. Cheloy had tents set up, knowing that they would prefer sleeping under the stars. Noli came over and shyly asked Caritas and Philip what they'd like to drink.

"A gin and tonic for me, and a red wine for the missus," Philip said heartily.

"You are so mid-west."

"But I *am* from the mid-west. Middle class and mid-west."

"Anyway that still makes you very First World. American middle class is Filipino filthy-rich."

"Did you know that the word "hooker" actually originated in the Philippines? There was this U.S. Army General by the name of Hooker stationed somewhere in the boondocks in the early 1900s and he was quite lax with his men. Allowed them all sorts of perks, so to speak. Bad for discipline."

"Perks like visits from sexually available Filipinas? For a fee?"

"The forerunners of the GROs. That's history anyway. I just thought it would interest you because it's about your country and all."

"Boondocks—that's another Filipino word. Like amuck. So that's what we've contributed—along with hooker, in a sense—to the English language. I can't say that makes me proud."

Noli brought their drinks over. On his way back to the house, Bart motioned to him and they spoke quietly. Then Noli set down his tray and followed Bart to another part of the beach. Shortly after, Melo came running out distractedly and with his last three buttons undone. He looked like he'd just used a facility.

"Have you seen Bart?"

"That way," Philip pointed to the opposite direction. Melo scurried off, his Birkenstock clogs sinking and letting in sand as he hurried along.

"You jerk! That was the wrong way," Caritas said.

"You really didn't want him to find them, did you? This is your niece's birthday party, right? You don't want any ugly confrontations. You have to think like a doctor, honey. First, do no harm. Besides, even the best couples occasionally need time away from each other, some breathing space."

"She's not really my niece. It's just a Filipino custom for young people to address their parents' friends that way."

"And what a lovely custom it is. Definitely more charming than the ninety different ways you have of saying homosexual in your language. What a country this is!"

The bonfire was burning brightly. The maids brought out trays of marshmallows and hotdogs so that the kids could have fun roasting them until dinner was served. Manolet Alba had large audio speakers set out on the verandah and announced that the cook and her husband would honor them by dancing a tango. They emerged, she still in her stained apron, and her toothless husband wearing faded and tattered shorts and battered topsiders. As soon as the music started, their subservient smiles transformed into expressions of stolid tragedy. Their heavy, gnarled and sunburned limbs twisted, spun and swayed with uncanny lightness across the stone tiles. Manolet and Dr. Sergio hooted and whistled to urge them on and they dipped and twirled madly in responses. Cheloy's friends laughed derisively but these indignities did not distract them from the primal rhythm and private passion of their dance. The young people, though, paid no attention to them and turned up their own music full blast.

"This is absolutely feudal, medieval, even," Philip sighed. "Come on, babe. I can't watch this."

"You think we're uncivilized. But they really do want to dance. They're not exploited just because they're servants."

"Kindness, honey, kindness. As William James said, the world could always use more kindness. Even when those who need it most don't realize it."

Philip and Caritas walked away from the bonfire. He found a low sand dune against which they could lean while they drank and watched the darkly glistening waves. As they sank down into the sand, there was a flurry of movement from the other end. Michelle and Don leapt out of the shadows.

"We were just talking," she squeaked. Don merely nodded. They stood about awkwardly for a while, then Michelle asked in a rush: "Tita Car, have you had dinner yet? But of course not—it's still too early. Well, see you later then. We'll join the others now." They scurried away.

Philip drew Caritas to him. She rested her wrists on his raised knees. He gently rubbed his cheek against her shoulder and nape. His fingers grazed lightly against the thick scars from her lumpectomy and cradled her breasts. The raftfull of boys, whom Michelle had been anxious about earlier, were gathered around the bonfire. They were very stoned and getting quite loud. One of the boys crept along the sand with his face so close to the flames that the others had to pull him back to keep his hair and eyebrows from getting singed. He claimed there was a secret configuration in the embers that would solve all the mysteries of the universe and he was the one chosen to reveal these. If they would only listen.

Caritas snuggled deeper against Philip. Her buttocks fit warmly against his crotch and his breath tickled pleasantly as he kissed her, over and over, in measure to the timeless lapping of the waves. She looked up and was mesmerized by the stars' diadem brilliance in the purple blackness of unsullied sky. This was proof enough that God existed, or as Philip had told her during mass the other day, that the kingdom of heaven is spread all around us even though men do not have the eyes to see. Over the last vestiges of the tango-techno mix, the young people's happy and excited voices floated, creating an ethereal music that Caritas imagined must be what the voices of angels sounded like. She found herself filled with the sense that now there was no mystery. This was forever.

Re: Torturing

REECH NODDED TO SERCH. It was a knowing, all-encompassing tilt of the head. In reply Serch raised his head and let his eyes open and close quickly. This typically fluttering response caused his long dark eyelashes to momentarily stick under his eyelids. He winced at the sensation and tried to flick the irritating hairs away from his eyes.

"Ow !"

Reech shook his head and pushed Serch's hands away from his face, delicately lifting the offending hairs from both eyes.

Their communication in this situation was usually whispered, their exclamations hushed accordingly, both out of respect for the dead and so as not to disturb the living

Reconciliation After Death requires all of its operatives to behave with the utmost decorum. While visual recognition by the living is unlikely it is not unheard of and as such the seriousness and importance of RAD's work would be compromised by inappropriate behaviour or vocal indiscretions.

"Shit…"

Reech punched Serch lightly on the arm. Serch opened his palms and shrugged his shoulders before pointing to the ground. His left foot had become embedded in a pile of soil that had been carelessly left to natural effect. It was a new graveyard, a new patch for the two operatives more used to granite and sandstone; Victorian hulks and death steeped in tradition. For five years they had been assigned the three cemeteries in the district covering the main denominations and they had gotten used to the routine, the ease of their jobs. Now, however, as the population grew a new graveyard had been opened, churchless and as Serch had sniggeringly pointed out, lifeless.

"There's no atmosphere to the place, Reech."

"Yes, its leaden…"

"Deadened, Reech, soulless and empty.

"Sure, but we go where we are sent, Serch."

"I know but I don't have to like it."

The first step was the call from the Operator, the local coordinator for RAD who assessed and determined which funeral services needed to be visited. Of course not every service was covered—this would stretch their resources too thinly and besides not every funeral would provide RAD with a suitable job. Some funerals were genuinely sad events, with hordes of family and relations queuing up to weep over the coffin, to soil their hands and to kiss the powdery cheeks of the nearest and dearest. Reech and Serch were never sent to these services. On occasion when the Operator gave them ill-informed direction, Reech and Serch would arrive at a well populated funeral, a tearful stream of mourners lining up to_pay their respects.

"Nobody wanted him to go," Reech would say

"He was loved and is missed." Serch would reply before wiping away a tear of his own, taking Reech's arm and walking out of the cemetery.

Most of the time, however, the Operator got it exactly right. The signifiers were there to be spotted by someone who knew what to look for. Local classifieds were the main source of information. Brief notices with no survivors listed and written in rest homes, dispassioned officialese were obvious possibilities but the Operator also cross-referenced entries in the death register with social reports to find particularly lonely and unwitnessed deaths. In addition scouring local papers could also prove useful since the death of a criminal or a disliked public official would often prove fertile ground for RAD's remit.

Their motto, emblazoned on all stationery and clothing was, "We Count the Tears."

Of course this motto was just the starting point and this was where operatives such as Reech and Serch came in. Arriving at a funeral, visual observations were key. When Reech had inducted Serch into the methodology of RAD his advice had been simple.

"Tears are not enough. Or rather you learn to distinguish between truly felt tears and the crocodile variety. You could hate the person being buried or cremated and still get caught up in the emotion of the ceremony as you imagine a loved one or even yourself being laid to rest. With a practised eye you can spot the difference. Sometimes there isn't a damp eye in the cemetery. All you do then is pick out the nearest and dearest, do some soul searching and you usually find a suitable candidate for some necessary reconciliation. At other times, you have to be observant and I mean observant. Look at the way they pick up the soil, watch the way they throw it, check who doesn't turn away and close their eyes when the coffin disappears behind the curtain on its way to incineration. Check the gaze, define the stare and understand how the simple curl of a lip can elucidate an inner pain, a tangible and destructive anger. That, Serch, is what we are here for."

Reconciliation After Death are a positive, life giving force. We take the living with all their pain and anger and direct them towards understanding. Death is not an insurmountable barrier with RAD; it is possible to say all the things that needed to be said and it is desirable that the bereaved do not have to live with regret.

Serch kicked impatiently at the pile of soil. It was typical that the newest cemetery should be so lackadaisical about grave gardening, as though once the mourners had gone it was unimportant to maintain standards. The minimum was all that was necessary. Still, their first job at the new cemetery seemed to be a textbook case, a mourner ripe for reconciliation. It showed all the signs as they moved closer to the graveside unseen and unheard by the stoic group huddled around the grave.

To begin with there were only five people there besides the undertaker and his staff. Three of the five stood back a certain distance from the grave which was tell tale as far as Reech and Serch were concerned. Their body language showed that they knew the deceased but not intimately and perhaps not even on a particularly friendly footing. Their distance depicted *distance*, either contrived or actual but either way there were no issues that needed reconciled. There were no tears certainly but neither was there any reason to believe that they were being painfully suppressed.

The fourth figure, a man of around 30 was holding the arm of another man roughly the same age. This was Esser Waite's son and sole survivor accompanied by what was most likely his closest friend. The friend was of no interest to Reech and Serch but the son, Uli, according to the Operator's fact search was prime material. Standing either side of him, nestled close enough to hear his breath, to put a finger to his eyes, Reech and Serch were unflinching in their concentration.

There were no tears. There was a curl of the lip. The soil routinely put into the son's hand stayed only for the briefest of moments—genuine mourners usually held on to the soil, tossing and turning it in their hands—and when he threw the earth at least three quarters of it missed the actual grave bouncing up the slope to the level ground. No one who was mourning would miss such a compelling target.

"He's our man, Serch."

Serch nodded, smacking his lips.

"Don't do that."

"What ?"

"That sound with your lips. Its off-putting and slightly distasteful."

"Sorry but I get excited when they are as easy to spot as this."

"Ah, but remember there's nothing easy about reconciliation. Otherwise people wouldn't need our services."

When the coffin was lowered, the mourners turned away and began to walk back up the freshly tarmaced road to the car park.

"Watch, Serch, there'll be a moment's hesitation and that will be our cue."

A few steps away from the grave, Uli patted his friend's arm and freed himself enough to turn his body back towards the grave. He nodded his head in the direction of his father but said nothing, his body stock still for a moment save the tightening of his right hand into a fist, the knuckles whitening with each passing moment.

It was the last he saw of the graveyard and his comforting friend.

The initial intervention between the deceased and the survivor has been known to startle, shock and in some cases atrophy the emotions of those involved. In its early years, Reconciliation After Death used a variety of locations usually linked to a common ground shared by the survivor and the deceased. These locations ranged from mountain tops to back bedrooms; from a rusting car to a walled garden. However, it transpired that these locations could distract from the purpose of reconciliation as the physical barred any progress with the spiritual and while one would be comfortable and shocked, the other would remain profoundly disturbed. As a result it was decided to minimise rather than symbolise. The canvas should be blank; the playing field level.

"A padded cell, Reech ? When did this happen ?"

"The powers that be decided that stone was too hard, too cold and too dangerous."

"Dangerous ?"

"For the reconcilees."

"So when it gets physical…"

"There is something to break their fall."

Reech and Serch were distinctive, black, straight lines in the white room. They were both tall, their 190 centimetres taking them close to the soft plastic material that bulged from the ceiling. In earlier locations their height had proved hazardous. For example their intermediation had taken them to an underground tunnel where the reconcilees arrived at either end of the low slung passage and with instinctive confusion and a typical deranged shock they had charged at each other, gaining speed over the 100 metre length of the tunnel, their voices screeching and echoing while Reech and Serch pressed themselves against the cold brickwork, closing their eyes, waiting for the collision, the fight and finally the silence where they could pick father and son from the ground and hold them till the shock diminished.

The padded cell did little to allay the heart-wrenching shock of impossible arrival but it cut down on injuries and saved valuable time for reconciliation. Time after all was important and far from infinite.

Research has shown that reconciliation after death is unlikely to occur over an extended period of time. Delayed shock, repetitive arguments and an increasing rationality about circumstance and situation will often cause the 'bereavement' bridge to crumble and in some cases disintegrate altogether. The Operator insists on reminding all operatives about this each and every time as there had been a few situations where both the deceased and the survivor had become stranded, a state of affairs that represented absolute failure and which threatened the very ethos and creed of Reconciliation After Death.

Uli arrived first. He filled in from top to bottom. Thin blond hair scraping over a furrowed brow, lank strands tickling thin lips of a mouth stretched in shock. Then the narrow shoulders and long arms supporting a mothballed suit down to spindly legs a five centimetre gap between hem and sock showing white skin, a flurry of fair hairs sprouting wildly outwards.

"Not exactly pin-up status, eh Reech."

"Its not for us to comment on the physical demeanour of the bereaved. It's irrelevant."

"Lighten up, Reech. Its possible to be lighthearted and grave at the same time. And this weasel of a man is one serious joke."

"Sometimes love comes in small packages."

"Sure…"

Serch broke off from his conversation and walked over to Uli whose whole body had begun to shake, his mouth loosening to emit a soft perhaps primal drone. Serch placed both his hands on Uli's shoulders and closed his eyes. Reech walked a few steps to the opposite corner of the room and stretched out his arms, palms facing the soft white floor. He too shut his eyes.

Operatives must be trained in Traumatic Stress Recovery. This is not a paramedic skill but a pscyhokinetic one, where using energy and tactile movement, the deceased or the bereaved may be assisted in their acclimatisation to their new environment. Spasms, screaming and incontinence are not uncommon by-products of transportation.

Esser arrived horizontally, his arms folded and crossed by the undertaker's assistant, his pallor enhanced by the same assistant's makeup kit. For a moment Reech stood looking at his empty palms, a look of irritation undulating across his face.

"Looks like they should have written 'This Way Up' on that one." commented Serch, opening his eyes at the same time as Uli."

Reech shook the irritation from his face and knelt down beside Esser, placing his hands on the old man's shoulders as he began to shake.

"Turn off." He said sharply to Serch, not wanting their voices to be heard by the new arrivals.

Serch backed away from Uli, his body now calm but his eyes were wild as they took in the white cell and he crossed the room to lay his hands on Esser's chest while Reech firmly gripped his shoulders. The old man was taking longer than his son to recover from the transport trauma. It was often the way. In a previous case an elderly woman had been unable to stop shaking or drooling for the entire contact period with her daughter but this hadn't stopped the reconciliation process. In a few short hours both Reech and Serch were moved to tears by the reconciliation. Where once there had been a bitter old woman and an exhausted, loveless daughter there were two people rejoined in care for each other. The daughter held her mother down with one hand and wiped away the saliva from her mouth with the back of her hand. Where there had been distance there was a necessary but unforced touch.

"They are nursing each other." Reech had said to Serch.

Expect the unexpected. There is no such thing as a doomed reconciliation. Our percentages are high at Reconciliation After Death and although not every case will work, both the deceased and the survivor are more likely than not to return to their own states. Even in extreme situations a sense of calm can be found; even within difficult physical circumstances that very physicality can be enough of a trigger for reconciliation. For operatives, the deceased and the survivor the motto must be Never Give Up.

When Uli unlocked he didn't see his father he only saw his hands which he spread over his face, the tips of his fingers pressing into his skin. It was the strangest sensation, like the feeling he'd had when his father had been working on an old lamp that lay at the back of the barn.

"Don't touch it."

And of course he had.

Uli remembered his father's shout, his own scream and the sudden immobility that came over his body. He was suddenly and painfully connected to the lamp. He watched its shade fall onto the ground but could do nothing to break the grip; he watched his hand take on a vibrating life of its own but could do nothing to stop it. It was only when his father hit his arm with an old piece of wood that the vibrating stopped and he and the lamp fell to the ground. First it was the smell he noticed, the singed, electrical charge that hung in the air—was there actually smoke? Then he felt his skin crawl and he looked at his arms expecting to see the skin rippling back and forward. Finally there was another blow, this time to his chest and in a moment his father was over him, the wires that he had so recently been connected to, being thrust into his face.

"Didn't I tell you not to touch it. You never listen, do you. You think you can do what you want and never mind the consequences."

Uli hadn't understood what had happened but he knew enough to know that if the bare wires his father held centimetres from his face touched him, it would all start again.

It would all start again.

WHEN ESSER OPENED HIS EYES he hadn't expected heaven. When he reached out and felt the cushions beneath him he hadn't expected soft. He'd thought about it often enough when the pain started to work its searing way through his body. He had already been a hapless witness to the death of friends at the home as they groped for meaning for both their lives and their dying. He rattled off platitudes and clichés, regurgitating phrases he knew were the wrong thing to say at the right moment but of course none of it helped him when his turn came. There was no one there to say it to him. The nurses at the home had been brisk in their reassurance, extending their hope for his survival no further than the next day. It was honest at least. The day before he died, no one had said a word to him, eye contact was avoided and the last thing Esser remembered was staring at the flaking paint on the ceiling of the hospital ward listening to the snores and moans of his fellow patients.

He had gone out with a whimper that wasn't even his.

Uli circled his father's body as it danced, his knees bashing against the soft cushions, his hands clawing, seeking grip. Here was an opportunity his father would have taken from first working memory to last tearless goodbye. As Uli lay sleeping, dreaming of something somewhere, in their cottage in the middle of nowhere, his father would decide when he should wake up. There was never any choice. Uli couldn't remember when he'd actually woken up of his own accord as a child. The time would change depending on the season but whether it was light or dark, Uli's entry to the day was accompanied by the sheets and blankets being rushed from the bed followed by his father's strong grip on his ankles. The floor was his welcome, his father's bark and bite his breakfast, the dizzying rush of consciousness his chore. Of course it was a hard life—little money, no mother to be known, isolated upbringing—Uli knew and had been told how to deal with all of that—but it was a life made harder by his father. 'Wrench out the pain' he had been told in later life, 'kindle and oxygenate the living, breathing flame of fire.'

It was always easier said than done. As a child in that wretched cottage, there was nothing done that was easy. He worked on what his father called the farm—rotting root vegetables and a few scrag ends of animals that whistled their breath in winter and stank to high heaven in summer—for hours that merged seamlessly with days, months and yes, a youthful lifetime. Once it had been a viable and managed workplace with his father selling produce to local markets and making a small but tidy living but when the mother he had never known had left him—'stolen in the night, she was, taken by stealth due to her health, let go without a sound or a fight.'—everything went to rack and ruin.

Then there was the drink. Uli knelt beside his father in the white cell and without looking into his eyes held an invisible glass or maybe a whole bottle over him and let it pour its soaking torrent onto his father's chest. It felt good. In his head he wanted to do that so many times. An eye for an eye. By the coffin in the graveyard it took a wild throw, a jerk in his arm to stop him dripping the sodden soil onto the coffin. If he had wrung his hands they would have dripped alcohol.

"You want some." He would say, " You wanna little drink ?" At the end of a long day that had started dark and ended darker, when there was nothing for him to do except sleep or watch his father, he had tried to close his eyes and scaffold his imagination enough for him to climb up, out and away. Except when he closed his eyes he could think of nothing to see, had not known anything to believe and anyway, of course, whatever, it was all changed when the drink would drip onto his face. Foul-smelling stuff that made him spit when it touched his lips. " Come on, it'll be good for you." When his father opened his mouth for him he did try to bite. 'Surely you must have fought back?' he was asked later. 'Surely as you got older you wouldn't take anymore of that...?' And, yes, he wasn't stupid, when he was old enough to think of a way out he took it but there were so many times when he shouldn't have been there and he was; so many times when he shouldn't have had the drip feed of alcohol and he did. When he bit, the hand soaked him, made him the lush he was from the age of eight. And he would find that a smack, a bruise and a rush of black was the only way out.

Reech tapped Serch's arm and they both moved away from Esser and Uli to a corner of the padded cell. Their tone as well as their voices muted.

"Doesn't look good, eh, Reech. The young one's got enough fire to burn hell and the old man's still got the shakes bad. "

"Ah, but you know how it goes at the beginning. The way it starts isn't usually the way it finishes.

"Sure but do you think we'll need to do the old switcheroo ?"

"I hope not, the operator said we'd used up our quota for this year already."

"The operator ! What does he/she/it know. They're not on the front line. We are."

"We'll see."

Reconciliation After Death aims to achieve results organically without resource to the complex and implicated tools at their disposal. However, on rare occasions when reconciliation is particularly problematic, transferrals are permitted. These transferrals allow the survivor and the deceased to exchange memories for a brief time. The transferral link is supervised by operatives and is used at their discretion. Not every transferral achieves positive results and depends on the willingness to comprehend the effect of these memories on the person concerned. To know what someone else thinks, in other words, is not to necessarily understand it.

Lint had probably been Esser's only friend. When his wife died he had travelled a good fifty miles to be with him and his infant son. Esser remembered it well. One moment he had closed the door on the ambulance as it sped away with his wife inside, wrapped up warm now that she had grown cold and the next he opened the door to be greeted by Lint who threw his arms around him, pushed him inside and told him, 'These are moments to blur.' And blur them they did. Esser had never been much of a drinker, a glass here and a bottle there but never anything extreme. Lint showed him otherwise. For a week they poured every conceivable liquid they could into their bodies so that, as Lint said, 'demons would come out.' They fought, talked and cried their way through the week. There was no time for sleep, no time for food only brief moments of sobriety where Esser would take stock of the chaos of his world, the screaming, hungry child, the disintegration of all things domestic and the ever growing pile of bottles and cans. Esser knew that these moments were his last attachment to life as he had known it, as he could possibly continue to live it. He had a chance then to wave Lint and his crates of booze goodbye and tend to his son, to his squalid life on the farm. Instead, Lint staggered from the rickety armchair, slapped him on the back and tipped a bottle into his mouth. "Life is for living!" he shouted loud enough to rouse Esser from his sober pause and loud enough to wake the young Uli in his cot.

Lint had never really left although of course he did. A week later he had gone back to the city; a month later he was gone from the country, resettled in a new life a fond farewell written in an unsteady hand.

As Esser lay dying in the rest home, other residents would stop by his bed and urge him to make peace with his past. "Do you have anyone to forgive," they asked, "Does anyone need to forgive you?" they also asked. But they only asked the question, they didn't wait for an answer. It was like the injections given by the nurses to make him feel better. They didn't wait around either to see the results.

There was Uli. Of course there was Uli. He had hardly been the father his wife would have expected him to be. He ripped through his son's childhood with the jagged edge of a bottle; raged and beat him for no reason but at the time it seemed there was every reason. He had worked him until his eyes had become hollowed-out sockets and these were still moments to blur and yet the closer he got to death the sharper they got into focus and there was nothing he could do about it. Letters and calls via the rest home came to nothing and he grew to understand that this death was his suitable fate.

Serch grabbed hold of Reech's arm anxiously.

"Time's running out, Reech, maybe we should use the transferral…"

"Wait…the moment's coming. You can tell. You can feel it."

ULI HAD STEPPED BACK FROM HIS FATHER partly to avoid being hit by his thrashing legs but partly because death had not taken away the smell of him that was all too familiar. He had left the cottage years ago without a backward glance and he had built a new life for himself in the city, with friends and a good job. There was hardly even a backward thought. A hardened grimace perhaps at Christmas time when his friends dwindled in number as they returned to their family homes; a twinge of something when his birthday came and he remembered more than the anniversary but whatever pain was coming rushing back to him now as he looked at his writhing pathetic father had scabbed over long ago. He had always said in lucid, bitter moments that his father had died a long time ago and yet…

And yet, he felt compelled to return to his side, pushed by something, maybe his heart, maybe the muscle-cramping tension building inside his body. He could no longer stand and he fell onto his knees, letting his father's feet kick back into him after all these years. And he didn't mind. He took the feet in his hand and held them as tightly as he could until the energy was drained from them. Then he took the arms and held them at the elbow first, working his way up to the hands which were clamped into fists which still aimed for his face. One by one he uncurled the fingers and pressed his own palms against the thin white skin, pushing until the punching stopped and his father's whole body was at rest.

His face was still contorted, whether in pain or anger or frustration he wasn't sure, but it was not a face he wanted to look at. He had seen it before in younger form and was repulsed by the expression. There was no love in it just as there had been no love in his life. Uli knew he could do nothing about that. He had lived the way he had lived, he had felt the way that he had felt and Uli could guess why this had been. He knew that his mother had died suddenly and tragically, he knew that the once prosperous farm had disintegrated into debt and dereliction and he knew that perhaps his father had been a proud man bent double by fate… Of course that was his problem, a problem he visited on his only son all too easily. But what was there left for Uli apart from all of this.

"Make peace," he had been told, "learn to forgive and not to regret." He had been advised by people who had never known death. And yet he felt unable to mirror his father's expression with his own emotions.

He pressed his hands onto his father's cold and clammy face and began to smooth out his features, forcing his jaw to relax, the eyes to unscrew and the teeth to unclench. When he lifted his hands he saw an expression he had never seen before. One of peace.

Reech hugged Serch in the corner of the padded cell but Serch didn't return the embrace. He seemed unsure.

"Is that reconciliation? Seems a little unresolved to me."

Reech laughed and propelled him towards Esser and Uli.

"Take a good look, Serch, sometimes there isn't a dramatic conclusion only a subtle beginning. Reconciliation isn't a parcel that can be wrapped and neatly tied up. It's both a practical bonding and a spiritual legacy. Our organisation is not offering absolution, that's not what we are here for. That comes later. Our job is simple. We reconcile even and especially after death. We were needed here for Esser and for Uli and, you know, I think somehow we'll always be needed. Anywhere. Everywhere.

LAKAMBINI A. SITOY

Shut up and live

MAN-HUNGRY, SHE'D CALL ME. *Desperado.*

Also, *ingrata, retrobada, simberguensa.*

In her mouth the words became names—of demons, black devils. I'd sit, facing the mirror, her stolen makeup running down my cheeks. The tears transformed my face into something awful, mythic, a creature from the outlands, living on wildcats and stalks of sugarcane.

It wasn't until years later, plodding through a college grammar book, that I divined their meaning. They were bastard Spanish, all that was left after four centuries, learned from enraged creoles and passed from father to daughter to sister to uncle to son.

And maybe it was true—I was ungrateful, dared talk back, could eat at her table without shame. All throughout my childhood she scolded me with a broom in her hand, scraping under the beds, dragging out rafts of dust and misplaced storybooks. From the backyard, as she hung up the wash, her voice cut through the fragrant morning, ordering me to practice my piano before the teacher arrived. "Your piano" she called the ordeal, which I had to survive each week beginning in kindergarten. (One day my parents had observed me happily gliding my fingertips over the strips of rattan on the sofa as I sung away; that Christmas a red toy piano arrived in the mail; the following year the upright was delivered in a crate. "It's what you wanted!" they exclaimed to my apprehensive face.)

We couldn't do housework because she'd read somewhere that it ruined talented hands, and since no maid would stay with her longer than two weeks, she suffered it herself. My aunts thought we were spoiled, reading all the time. In our Character Education picture books the little girls washed dishes and scrubbed floors, wearing identical mini-dresses. "More industry!" the aunts declared, but they were lower class, weren't they? Their children didn't have *our* study habits.

I fell from her grace when I was 10. It began when my marks went down and I started snitching her cosmetics. The dresser in their bedroom was cluttered with bottles and jars, unopened for years. Some had gone off in the heat. I loved the fat greasy pencils the color of a pale sea. I covered my sister Tanya's lids in them and found a matching dress in the depths of my mother's closet. My own eyes I lined with black. We got into the perfume. Some bottles I borrowed without asking.

But "my piano" wasn't improving; my repertoire, for evening guests, consisted of the same stilted minuets. Gradually helping out in the kitchen ceased to be a game—it joined the ever-growing list of my duties. We were truly spoiled, as the aunts declared; I'd discovered my mother's Harlequin romances, and nothing could budge me on a Saturday morning. So my mother did all the chores while the aunts searched the barrios for household help.

One afternoon when I was 13, coming in late from school, I found her on the rattan sofa, waiting, her eyes gleaming in the half-light. She grabbed my wrist and sniffed at my hair. Exhale, she commanded, and drew back at the odor of tobacco and breath mints. I'd spent an hour behind the Practical Arts building with two boys a year older. Aldon had pimples and the kind of skin color that gets dismissed as black. He'd told dirty joke after dirty joke, sniggering with self-importance, turning to his friend for feedback. Ray was cool. He never smiled, just took thoughtful drags on his cigarette, bending, proffering the end of it so I could light my own, his silky black hair brushing my eyes.

Probing my satchel, Mama found my Winstons, my butane lighter, her eyeliner, her perfume, and the three joints Ray had asked me to hold for him so he could pass security check unmolested. His name and picture were in the gate guards' log: number three on the list of troublemakers. Sometimes they frisked him for knives, checked his knapsack for lengths of pipe, before they let him into the school compound. Or on a whim they searched his possessions for official property: the innards of an intercom or stuff like that.

Mama leafed in stony silence through my spring-back notebooks. Examined the notes scrawled in the margins to seatmates, the drawings of naked women in ankle-strap shoes.

"You know how you look to me?" she said. "A man-hungry whore."

That week and all into summer I lost my allowance. It left me no choice but to lie in bed picking through trashy novels, glaring as my younger sister counted *her* money. Limp brown ten peso bills, the occasional orange twenty. Tanya padded the wad with stiff paper dollars from the Monopoly tray, holding it up to her nose and **inhaling** deep, unaware of my disgust.

"I'm getting out of here," I told her. "When I'm 18, I'm taking my money and hiring a stud. I'll get the biggest, buffest, dumbest stud I can find and then I'll fuck him."

She stared at me in fear, clutching the bills as though afraid I might snatch them from her.

"And after that I'm running away. I'll take the first plane to the States."

She snorted. "Mama would never allow you."

ONE EVENING SOME YEARS LATER, I sat down in the sala opposite my mother, choosing the rattan peacock chair, and told her I was pregnant.

She was correcting test papers on the sofa. Her feet were up on a cushion because her cheap shoes pinched. As always, I was affronted by the prettiness of her legs—the pale brown skin, the long toes, as on the statue of a saint. You would not have guessed, to look at her face. I wanted those feet down, safe beneath her hideous batik skirt; I wanted contradictions out of the way.

"Ma, I need an abortion," I said, and started to cry.

Her features aged a decade. She did not speak. I told her about the sore breasts, my bladder bursting in the mornings, the period that never came, though I had prayerfully pasted a sanitary pad to my underwear for seven mornings running. Deep within me a force had accelerated my heartbeat and invaded my throat with a new and constricting rhythm. I fell silent, and still she didn't speak. *Look*—sobbing anew—*I have money.* I pulled out my wallet. In it was four thousand three hundred fifty pesos—-culled from my allowance, and the remainder of a prize I had won last year, for writing the best essay out of all the college students in the city. Look, I can pay for it myself, I said. I have a doctor in mind. I know where to go. I know what it will cost.

Her eyes bulged, her shoulders humped in defeat. She watched me weep. She could not find words. I had shut her up. For once.

"What does Eric have to say?" she managed at last.

"I'm never going to tell him."

But of course the father already knew—last night he had walloped me across the face, so hard that I fell across the dank bedspread in his rented room, my head hitting the lawanit wall with a thud. This was for even mentioning the procedure. If I went through with it, he swore, he would put both his hands around my throat and choke the life out of me. Then he'd barred the door. In here I would stay until the baby was much too big to be extricated without killing me as well. As I'd struggled to get past him, I'd called out for help, once, just once, and the radio in the next room had fallen silent, but none of his housemates had come to my aid.

"He is not involved," I sobbed, and put my arms to my face. My mother saw the blue bruises below my wrists. At this her pain flared into anger—"But *why* did you have to do this? How *could* you, Narita!" Abruptly she diverted her attention to the fourth-grader test papers. She began to check them, slashing red marks into the pulp with her pen. "I thought you had reformed. I thought you were a good girl. How could you *do* this to us?"

My mother never asked questions, until it was too late, and answers were moot. By then what queries she summoned sounded like indictments—Why didn't you phone us? Why do you have to play with that dirty boy? What were you doing in the bathroom for an hour?

She did it best before an audience, waiting for suppertime and the arrival of my father and sister and whichever uncle or aunt was sleeping in the spare room.

She knew, and we knew, that she was made for better things—lawyering, prosecution, attack. Instead, half her life had been spent in the cul-de-sac of a private elementary school, where she was Second Mother to the children of the city's doctors and gentleman farmers. Her ultimate reward, for years, was a class of 40 pliant, attentive 10-year-olds, hands folded on their desks, chorusing "Good *bye,* Mrs. Kastur!" at 4:25 p.m. each day, as school children in our city have done since the days of American instruction.

She'd hit me for talking back—never on the cheek, never a swinging, stylish Hollywood slap, but square on the mouth, winding her arm around to get me with the heel of her hand. Mashing my upper lip against my nostrils, blinding me. Like running clumsily into a wall. That seemed to be the point. Stupid girl, why don't you look where you're going? Once I saw her take an eight-year-old by the face. She grabbed him and pressed his cheeks between thumb and index finger, forcing his jaws apart, so that he sat there, eyes rolling to the ceiling, molars on display.

MY MOTHER GAVE IN WITH A PASSIVITY that astounded me. Just as we heard the car pulling into the driveway—Papa returning from an evening meeting— she said, "You'll have to go to Cebu for it, I can't have you visiting a doctor in this city."

A couple of days later, I packed a change of clothes into a worn denim knapsack and bought a ticket on the overnight boat to the next island. My sister rode with me in the pedicab, a silent presence as we walked the concrete pier, keeping to the side, away from speeding forklifts. I felt her hating me, not for the abortion to come, but for the disloyalty of sleeping with Eric. We had second-class tickets, which meant we would spend the night on sticky green canvas cots down in the hold, near the waterline. The odor of tar, an eternal feature of the docks, made me violently ill, and I clung to the railing greasy from a thousand other hands, which left its own rusty-metal scent imprint on my palm. The boat edged away from the pier, and, as when I was a little girl and making this journey for the first time with my father and mother and Tanya, I looked down at the black ocean, and at the froth, green-white in the ship's lights, that slopped past as we cleaved the waves. The thrill was in staring into that glass-green until jumping was inevitable. Always I pulled back: chicken.

The ship was an aging vessel that had began life in Japan, ferrying freight and passengers from one island to the other. The toilets were porcelain trenches in a wet and muddy floor. On the walls, the survival instructions were a cipher no one here would ever crack. Dragging myself away from the railing, I stumbled over bags and great bails of noodles. The hallway space had been halved by a row of occupied cots that the shipping company hoped would increase profit. There were so many people on this vessel; there were too many people in the world. I found my place, in the chilly compartment where, like Tanya, a hundred others were already prostrate, closing their senses to the thrum of the motors and the suffocating nearness of fellow humans. A steward went around absently tossing thin cotton blankets onto each cot. He was thin and dark and bore a resemblance to Eric, in the full lips and soft round chin, the fleshy thrusting nose. He even had a little mustache.

He was face number four: The Priapic Brochero. In her sophomore year in Fine Arts, Tanya declared there were only six Filipino faces, and then proceeded to sketch each one. Prominent cheekbones here, a shelf of brow bone there, a mouth filled with healthy white teeth. Face Number Three. The

Pensive Tikbalang. She was extremely inventive. Face Number Five. The Sleepless Mandarin. And so on.

I shrieked with laughter at her daring. You racist! She cast me a look of impatience that nonetheless had an implicit plea for mercy, because she was younger by two years, and I could mock this latest passion into oblivion, as I'd done with her stamp collecting and her dream of acquiring a high-end, liberal Scandinavian husband. "I'm not a racist," she said. "Look around. I simply record what I see."

That entire night I sat, looking around indeed, at the men and women on either side, innocent in their sleep, unaware of the caustic eyes that examined their every feature, their scabby feet, their worn denims, the precious purses they clutched to their chests, the Walkmans that soothed them through the darkness of their dreams. Every age, every infinitesimal degree of disappointment, was represented here.

The creature's presence registered as a queasiness in the pit of my stomach; I sucked on one sweet after the next, but as soon as my mouth was empty, gastric juice and garlic from my latest meal arose, grain by grain surfacing at the top of my throat, invading my sinuses and my nostrils. *It* was a mistake, I could not possibly love it. As it slept, tucked within the membranes of my abdomen, it fired bitter chemicals into my bloodstream. Tissues divided, flesh grew, with my every breath. What features resided within the bud of its face? It was as though Eric lay clenched within me, sniggering, his violent phallus growing past his forehead, his hands similarly out of proportion, curling occasionally into the iron fists I knew so well.

TANYA AND I, WE TOOK A TAXI FROM THE DOCKS to the abortionist, reading out the address from the slip of paper in my hand. The office was in a featureless concrete building from the 70s. It had elevators. It was the elevators that made the place remarkable. In Buglasan, nothing was taller than five stories.

I punched all the buttons, playfully, to show Tanya the situation did not deserve such a long face. What could be so tragic, when we were having fun.

We jolted to a stop at each of the eleven floors. "Stop it," my sister said. Tanya thought I was being heartless; she hated Eric with a vengeance, was jealous of all my boyfriends, but a pregnancy was something else.

"*Pagpuyo!*" she added, and that sobered me up. *Puyo* means "live," *pagpuyo* an order to exist, quietly; to "stay," like the dog command.

The hall had carpeting. It was one of the few times I had been in a carpeted hallway. There was something decadent, glamorous about spending a huge amount of money on a medical procedure. As we walked to the end of the hall, I was not afraid. I had no guilt, no thoughts of God. Religion had never been much of a factor in our lives anyway.

The doctor was the biggest abortionist in Cebu. She'd survived, year upon year, through the whispered words of women, always beneath the official radar. She came from an old family and was too rich and well-placed for the authorities to catch her—if indeed in all those years anyone ever complained.

I didn't know what to expect. A woman in flower prints, with the gushing mien of a kindergarten teacher? Science fiction expanses of white? The waiting room was cramped, like a dentist's clinic. The plants were real—Tanya checked —ugly succulents like what my mother raised. The seats were upholstered in granite and green. The receptionist was one of those chatty, homey types, as though determined to surmount the unfriendly surroundings. She was probably only in her 20's. Which one of you is the patient? she said, and a look of shock passed over my sister's face.

I gave my real name. I felt no shame. We sat down on the hard green cushions. Tanya had brought *The Razor's Edge*, me, *Sister Carrie*. Those were the books we read in those days. Paperbacks bound in black and gold, gouache cover art, from the 1960s. We borrowed them from the American family down the block, from the university library, from my father's friends. We knew they were important. We were desperate to read, to educate ourselves, be different.

After a page each, we exchanged books. A few minutes later, we swapped again. It was useless. I told myself this was no worse than a root canal. I'd had a root canal when I was 18. I'd fainted, but survived. Tanya had drawn it, on the thick sole of her tennis sneaker, in ballpoint. She crossed her legs, *de quatro*, left ankle on right knee, her eyes fierce, to show me her work. Four weeks? Eight weeks? What difference did it make? A nub with eyes, somatic buds, a tail. Nerveless as tooth pulp.

The doctor was vexed, somehow, when I came in, and I wondered if I'd done something wrong. She couldn't have been very old, but when I tried to smile nothing registered behind the lenses of her huge glasses. She wanted to know if my periods were regular. If I'd had intercourse with anyone in the last three weeks. How often, and how many days ago exactly.

The entire sordid history of my sex life to date, which I had withheld from my mother, spilled out with the tears. In his boardinghouse bed. On the beach. Against a tree. Two months, three months, six months ago. Eric hated condoms, hated the expense, but liked to carry one nonetheless, the same one, unused through date after date. Once at a Xerox machine he had reached absently into his pocket for some change and instead pulled out the Sultan in its square plastic package. "I thought it was a ten-peso bill," he told me with a smirk afterwards. He'd handed the condom to the copier boy, who snickered, because he made it his business to exchange philosophies with the students who hung around his machine, buying cigarettes a stick at a time and menthol candies afterwards to get rid of the smell. He was well-acquainted with Eric and had heard about all the girls he had spied on through cracks in shower room walls, gaps in bamboo fences. Later, the transaction over and the mistake sorted out, this man, this worthless father-to-be, swaggered away, grinning wide enough to show his purple gums.

The doctor was not amused.

There were no lab tests, not even one of those two-blue-line urine processes that, years later, I came to know quite well. "No question of it," the gynecologist said after my recitation, having noted down a few dates. "You are pregnant." A pause, which seemed rehearsed. "Now. What do you want us to do with it?"

They wouldn't let Tanya into the inner sanctum, which was walled off with accordion pleats. I caught her eye and shook my head, begging. The receptionist took her by the arm and pulled her, firmly, out into the waiting room.

The cot had a rubber sheet. When the doctor probed me with a gloved finger that was slicked with some clammy gel, I closed my eyes. The finger became an implement. As I lay there watching the buzzing fluorescent panel overhead, I felt my vagina become a channel to mysterious chambers, one following the next, chambers I had never been aware of before, now clamped apart and explored with cold steel.

Apparently satisfied that all my innards were normal, she left the anteroom. I lay there far longer than I would have wanted, listening to the clink of instruments, of water running in the chamber beyond. I had no thoughts. It was silent—the creature whose heartbeat had flickered in my throat. There was no sensation in my gut, no sourness at the back of my tongue. The secretary came in and it was she who named the sum. The doctor evaded the indelicate issue of money. When I nodded to show her I accepted, she handed me a small cup of clear plastic. In it, three white pills rolled out of their blister packs, so I could not tell what they were.

"They're Tylenols," she whispered. "Two of them. The third is some other pain killer."

"No injections?" I whispered back. "No anesthesia?"

She shook her head. "They're all you need. It's a small procedure. A blood clot, really. Don't worry, she does this all the time."

WAS THAT WHAT MADE ME CHANGE MY MIND? Was I scared of pain, of blood, the sectioning of flesh, was that all?

Maybe it was the detachment of the whole procedure, maybe it was because the guilt-trip I had been expecting, like a Christian counseling hotline only face-to-face, didn't seem forthcoming. Maybe it was the look of distaste the doctor gave me when, a few seconds later, she peered past the curtain and found me in tears.

"How old are you?" she said. "Twenty? Twenty-five? Last week we had a girl in here. Fourteen years. She didn't cry and neither should you."

Factors converged. If my sister had not been outside that door, shame-faced, angry, but also extremely clinical, I would have gone through with it. Vacuumed her out. Dilation and curettage. Tanya saved her. I made up my mind, on that doctor's table, that if my sister had come this far, was faithfully waiting in the corridor, her knapsack bulging with the sanitary pads she feared we would need, she would be there the rest of our lives. The third point in the triangle, pillar of an odd new family.

I got off that table. Kicked my legs out of the stirrups. Mumbled apologies as I retrieved my clothes.

"Why is she leaving?" the doctor said. "What did you tell her?"

The women stood by in silence as the miracle, the happy ending, the poster girl for the pro-choice lobby—for indeed wasn't a child a choice?—blundered out of the clinic, not even saying goodbye.

"Oh God, it's done," Tanya said, rising at the sight of me pale and shaking, exultant.

In the taxi I told her. She threw her body into the air and landed, hard, on the upholstery, so that the driver checked his rear view in alarm.

"STUPID!" SHE SAID. "Jesus."

And then we shopped. We ordered the driver to take us to the largest department store he knew. We threw away my money, my contest prizes, months of accreted allowances. Ripped, cropped tops were back in fashion that season; I took two of those, and a pair of stretch denims that I reasoned

I would fit into next year, and funky sneakers, and some ragged lacy stuff for my hair. I bought Tanya some fragrant oil pastels in a wooden case.

We were ravenous, drowning—girlhood's last gasp, or a frantic attempt to deny what was on its way. Our third sister. Our daughter. Only the merest flicker at the base of my throat, a minute force that held back the tide of my blood.

⊕   ⊕   ⊕

As it was, I didn't love her. If there could have been a way, to send her back, to keep her from pushing her insistent way into the world. Go away, Naia. Shrivel. Shrink back into a wet pulsing mass of pink, into what you were in the first unknowing hours after I made you; go back to the beginning, membrane by membrane, protein by protein, until you are one with my tissues again, until you are no more.

In my memory box, a collection of anomalous images—a greenish-white interplay that defies logic, for they are of Naia getting born. I cannot for the life of me imagine why they come in such clarity, for as far as I know I was completely out of it: flat on my back, drugged, praying for liberation from the creature in my body. There I am, a pathetic 200-lb bulk beneath a white sheet, the center of me risen like a yeast bubble, my legs in the stirrups.

Then I am rising, out of myself, registering the rubber-gloved hands of the doctor now, aware of sounds. Deep, lowing noises reverberate through the delivery room and the halls beyond: they are me, my cries of birthing distress.

Between my spread legs, Naia's skull, grey with fine plastered hair—the moment of crowning. My daughter rips through the curtains of my sex, sliding her fine body out—at birth already an athlete, already possessing the face she is to wear through adolescence, but flattened, compressed, unsunned: a viscid present knowing air for the first time. She has my father's brows, my grandmother's hairline. The gynecologist hoists her up by the ankles. She swings. Her eyes, black beady slits, survey the world. There is life, there is terror in their depths.

Nothing else follows. I must have rushed, appalled, back into my own body at that point, unable to face this creature, this hungry new organism— a fetus with a will.

I wake up, and Naia is in the nursery down the hall. She is powdery white and pink, I am to learn later, while all the other infants in the ward are the usual terra cotta. Although she is only a day old, it is obvious she is blessed. I descend into feigned sleep, dreading the moment I will have to hold her in my arms.

AND NOW 18 YEARS HAVE PASSED, and I am a different woman, in a different city, bearing a new last name. The triangle of myself, my sister and my daughter spans oceans and seas. Over us hovers the figure of my mother, mellowed with age but very much alive, providing soundtrack and vocabulary—a voice that never leaves my head, although I have instructed myself time and again to wipe the tape.

The distance is fiction. We are in touch. Of sorts. My sister sends me brief, occasional e-mails from a place called Sprowston, where for a year and a half she has lived in a flat shared with two other Filipinas. Silent Mandarins and Pensive Tikbalangs are gone from her life. When she discovered she couldn't raise a baby on the income from pencil sketches, she went to nursing school instead. I left even before she made this choice—for Manila, to find a job. But the jobs available to a college dropout who'd read a lot and could write a little paid barely enough for my room and board, and so it was Tanya who bore the consequences, silently and furiously, of my two moments of weakness—it was she who raised my daughter, until she too left to seek her fortune.

It is a rainy Friday and Quiapo traffic is at its worst. Two kilometers before the church, the line of stalled commuters begins. The pavements are slicked with brown pulp from hundreds of grinding wheels. The road is a giant alimentary canal; we move, boluses of humanity, in pulses, a car length at a time. I ponder Tanya's last, frantic e-mail—*I don't believe it. You must verify. She would never!*—and fight nausea, the urge for violence.

Desperate for movement, I unlock the door and ease myself into the steaming air.

I slip past stalls selling roots and drying greens. Abortifacients, cures for impotence. Vendors crouch beside displays of movie star magazines, chrysanthemums for the dead, brass fertility amulets, mobile phone cases, cigarette lighters with naked women on them, lucky red seeds to adorn the wrists of newborn babies, playing cards, pirated music, stolen watches, prawn chips, fish curls. Losing my way, I find myself almost upon the church before I have the sense to retrace my steps, ducking my head, my knapsack clutched against my ribs, blundering down a side street. Wads of new spit shine on the asphalt, like medals.

I find the hawkers of video CDs soon enough. At the first stall I ask the girl guarding the merchandise for a copy of "Boarding House" and she reaches carefully beneath her display table. She is about 20, egg-smooth and fair, hair drawn back into a ponytail, a mat of sweaty strands marring her nape.

I glance quickly at what she hands me: the title printed in electric pink letters, the accompanying images, in montage, mostly of naked skin.

I take the first available ride home.

No one is about when, nearly two hours later, I get to the house. The two maids are outside the gate snipping fresh growth off the san franciscos, but they don't count; I've avoided my parents-in-law again—blessed relief. Showering the commute off me I boot up the computer. My breathing is even. Out of habit, I keep my face devoid of emotion, even behind the locked door where no one can see.

Extricating the VCD from my satchel, I look it over, daring myself to run it, puzzling over the text: the words Boarding House in pink, the word Hole in acid green, and two more words, For Rent, in vibrating cyan. Which is the title and which is the tag line? Are the words supposed to travel, pair up as I see fit? The words shuffle around by themselves—

Boarding house for rent.

House hole.

Hole rent.

Then I slip the movie into the computer. My hands shake; my fingers slide on the keys. Cursing, I search the icons on the screen, looking for a program that will run the video. This is my property but I have not used it for weeks. It's now a repository for my husband's night-long downloads.

At last, a window materializes onscreen, and then, an image, a hand.

It fills the screen. Thin and knuckly, knowing its business. Two fingers plunge, in and out, of a whorl of black hair. The hand is a knife, it is a fist, it punches this ancient face, stabs it, meets the bucking hips, pommels the faintly oily ridges of its secret features.

The camera pulls back, to reveal the body. The sharp breasts, the taut mouth. The eyes that look straight into mine.

My daughter sees me.

Then the room dims. I double over, race for the bathroom, am sick—gastric climax—on the tiles.

HOW DOES IT GO, THE JOKE? Let me see if I can remember it, for I heard it only once, from Ray, beautiful, criminal Ray, who cursed me out loud for losing the joints he'd asked me to hold. I'd been too frightened of him to admit that my mother had destroyed them. He flayed me in the hallway between Biology and Statistics, and his classmates laughed.

It's not the sort of joke you'd easily forget—

Once there was a man who was extremely ugly. His skin was pitted and as sooty as the bottom of a clay pot, and on his nose and chin and shoulders and back were blemishes, which, at the point of breaking, were a pearly color, like grains of rice. His eyes started from his face. His teeth were peasant teeth, too big for his mouth, like naked wedges of garlic. His legs were stumpy. His hair curled.

Miserable, unloved, he climbed to the top of a mountain and contemplated the rocks below. At that moment an angel appeared to him. "Before you do anything stupid," the creature said, "listen. You are awful to look at, but your heart is relatively pure, and so we're giving you a chance, the chance to transform yourself into anything, anything in the universe you would want to be. Jump off that ledge over there. It's an enchanted ledge. As you go over, shout out the name of what you wish to become, and see what happens at the bottom."

The man's face lit up and he scrambled over to the spot that the angel had indicated, but in his eagerness, he slipped on a loose stone and tumbled off the edge. "Ay, *bilat!*" he yelped, and that's what he was by the time he landed, *thplok!* a huge and slurping *bilat*, a cunt cradled neatly between two rocks, scrubby with hair, clitoris pointing like a pink stinger to the sky.

IN THIS DREAM, I AM WITH HER AGAIN. I speak her name, two mellifluous syllables—Naia. The language is different, the landscape sun and sea. The city of my childhood, the city where I left her. Her hair slips out of the twin knots into which I have twisted it. Damp and greasy in the salt air. Drool slicks her lower lip like strawberry gloss. She wears tiny red boots with white fur trim and a little gold chain, and her face is clenched in misery as she stumbles across a sun-flooded tarmac, an airline boarding pass clutched in one hand. She looks up and sees me dutifully waving, belted into my seat even before the stewardess does the routine check; she is coming to me; no, she is here to say goodbye. Naia is two hundred yards away, behind the safety of a steel fence, held high in my sister's arms. The white of her small palm and a spot of red leatherette. 'Bye mommy.' The aircraft pauses a moment at the end of the runway, then is flung forward, past ditches of succulent gabi, tethered goats, a carabao, a tricycle loaded with nipa fronds. A single overwhelming moment of weightlessness, then the press of the entirety of sky on my forehead and breastbone. I lean, intoxicated, toward the window, toward the tilting horizon, filming mental footage—the corrugated blue of ocean, the spindly outrigger craft of fishermen, the sprinkling of blazing zinc roofs. Bye bye.

Hunger now, gnawing; and five-star hotel sandwiches. Delicate cold cuts with the crusts sliced off the bread. The cool surprise of lettuce, which I have tasted once or twice and never forgotten. My destiny is changing, I will it so; the adventure that is Manila stretches before me. I rocket out of my life, traveling farther and farther away from my daughter, now only an after-image with palm in the air. Forever fixed behind that restraining fence, she can't move, can't follow, must wait until I see it fit to come back.

And then, as half-dreams go, this one takes a strange turn at the moment of exultation: the stewardess with her trolley begins to travel in slow motion backward; the aircraft lists and I find myself looking up at my bent thighs; light pours through my skin; we tumble, silently and inexorably, toward the vast sea.

THIS IS NOT A DREAM. I am with her again, I am home. It is the last week of May, the month of extremes, of burning sun and torrential rains and, in between, the humidity that no amount of fanning can relieve. The shame of exposure confines her to her bedroom, dreading the eyes, the neighbors craning their necks to get a glimpse of her through the gumamela hedge. What a story to tell their friends. "We live next door to the x-rated whore. She goes around the house stark-naked."

At night, when my parents are asleep, Naia steals out for a few minutes to forage through the refrigerator, escaping with a bowl of cold rice and a link of chorizo maybe, mutely depositing a crusted plate in the sink. I've caught her tonight, cramming food into her mouth with her fingers: she eats only once, twice a day. The harsh white light overhead brings out the heavy shadows beneath her eyes. Her chin is a pointed little V, startling on a face I always remembered as round. She wears the patterned pajamas and little white t-shirt of a child at a slumber party; a line of pink studs describes a tiny heart across her chest. In the daytime I hear her sobbing. I can't look at her, can't take this plaintive, adult emaciation.

We sit across from each other, two strangers, fighting the realization that there is nothing we can say. My questions begin with Why. Why did you do it? Why did you date him? How could you have trusted him? We gave you everything, how could you have done this to us?

He stuffed you; I saw how much you loved it.

Did you know there was a camera mounted in the wall?

And if you did—

In my exasperation I want to choke her, squeeze the truth out of her young defiant throat. You cunt, talk to me.

It is close to midnight now. Gossamer insects beat at the fluorescent bar over our heads. They fall, broken-winged, to the kitchen table, wriggling, trying to navigate the obstacle of our sweat-filmed arms. Each year they materialize with the first rains of the monsoon, stay a couple of weeks, then disappear.

Flowers at the bottom of a cliff, we stare into each other's faces, silent, stoppered in our shame.

☸

TONI DAVIDSON

Like a Pendulum in Glue

I DON'T WANT TO BE HERE.

Louche screwed his eyes tight shut. He pressed his fingertips into his eyes and tried to chase the lingering orange blotches away from the darkness. For a few seconds he could still see the strip light until its glow slowly faded into nothing. He was lifted on to the kitchen units while the voice, his voice, kept repeating *I don't want to be here, I... don't... want... to... be... here.*

BRING IT ON BABY, LET THE GOOD TIMES ROLL.

Louche heard his father singing, an off-key rendition, a vibrating sore that pulsed and throbbed, burrowing deep into his head. The tape was blasting in the empty kitchen and although he couldn't see him, Louche could hear his father's dance steps, tapping and scraping at the vinyl floor. His father was a good mover. Sometimes when Louche's eyes were half-open, that frightening slit of light searing his world, halting for a moment his voice, he had seen the quick steps, the body swerves and hip sways. His father was in no doubt of his own abilities. In half vision Louche saw him linger in front of his image in the long mirror which hung on the wall. He swerved and veered in front of it, checking his step every so often to twirl then sweep a can from the floor, a swift drink that didn't break his tempo.

LET'S SHAKE, SHAKE, SHAKE.

Louche kept his eyes closed even when he heard his father tap his way closer to him, his hands keeping time with the rock 'n roll beat, drumming an

68 ❀ Toni Davidson

insistent rhythm on the kitchen surface, a vibration that rippled his skin and made the hair on his arms stand up.

COME ONE BABY WON"T YOU DANCE WITH ME.

The words were both in the air and in Louche's face. His father took Louche's bony arms and swung them from side to side but still, he kept his eyes shut, not letting one ray of light into his head. The voice inside was still there, he didn't have to check to make sure. It never seemed to go away.

I want to be somewhere else.

Suddenly the music stopped and he felt his father lean forward. His words were whispered, a long breath taken in and slowly released.

"Son, you have to learn to enjoy yourself."

"C'mon baby, come closer."

Louche's eyes were wide open in the pitch black. And he could see nothing. She wasn't talking to him. Louche knew that. But for a strangely dark and sparkling moment he thought she was. Who she was talking to, who in fact *she* was, Louche had no way of telling in the blackened arch. He sensed her close to his body, not just her scent but that sense of movement that doesn't require vision—like his own voice which didn't need to be spoken. Of course, he could have reached out and touched but his heartbeat quickened and a voice in his head surged.

Take a step back, move away from this corner, get back into the open.

For a moment he hesitated, just enough to feel another presence close to him, brushing past his near-naked body. Scent, movement and yes, expectation told him that it was a man. Louche pressed himself tightly against the wall he knew was behind him and the woman's insistent encouragement first faded then became muffled, her voice swallowed by a kiss, the sound of flesh against flesh, the sigh of release…

Inside, Louche could hear a voice again, its tone pulsing with threat, its persistent echo refusing to fade until he listened, obeyed and once again squeezed his eyes half-shut and groped his way along the wall and into the next arch.

IT WAS A LITTLE BRIGHTER, illuminated by the lash of candlelight. Here, the dozen or so figures moved as though exercising some kind of penitence. A slow walking monotony weighed down their steps, their bodies rigid and shackled by chains, but their heads and particularly their eyes were alert to their surroundings. Their clothing was elaborate but not particularly sophisticated. Stretches of rubber held by stretches of skin. Some men had rubber masks, some women thigh-length boots. It was uniform. In front of him an overweight, middle-aged man was led by an erstwhile dominatrix, chain in one hand, a whip dangling limply by her side. The entirely neutral look on the man's face terrified Louche, galvanised his own self-reproachment into a frenzy, dragged him over burning coals, each with a spike that drove deep into his flesh, making his skin pop and sigh. Near one of the elaborate candlesticks that lit the poor brickwork of the arch a man leaned against the wall, his hands behind his head, his eyes shut tight, a grimace of something on his face. On her knees a woman dressed as in Victorian times was sucking his penis, her quickening, thrusting movements dislodging her emerald green hat, the veil temporarily shifted to one side. There was a strange routine not only to their action but to the others in the room, single men mostly who watched with tight lips where lips were visible, with concentrated stares where eyes could be seen. But for the distant thud of music there was silence in the room broken only by the metal links of the dominatrix's chain.

What is the point of this? I should be the point of this.

The other voice inside him, the one that rose above doubt's persistent echo flashed like a torch in darkness. It reminded him why he was here. For a moment, just for one teasingly succinct moment. Until he felt overwhelmed by hope's bright glare, until he felt as though he was suffocating and unbearably hot, despite his near-naked state. Clothed only in rubber shorts and leather boots he felt restricted and, at the same time, both under and over dressed. He shut his eyes completely, not wanting to be part of the silent stare, not feeling he had anything to share.

"COME ON LET IT FLY, LET IT GO..."

His father gave him the kite just as it gained some height. He was jogging backwards up the hill, struggling and fighting with the string, both laughing and cursing as it dipped then soared then dived towards the ground, its brightly coloured tail close to the grass. As it climbed again, Louche closed his eyes and hung on to its tail, feeling the lift and rise into the air, his own dangling legs becoming part of its tail. He was jogging half-heartedly alongside his father who was willing and wishing the kite into the air. For one moment his father unexpectedly lifted him up off the ground desperately trying to give the kite a chance to fly in the light wind. When he lifted him up, Louche opened his eyes just the tiniest of fractions and saw the ground rush away from him. For that moment he too was airborne. But then the kite nose-dived and he too found himself back on the ground, his father huffing and puffing beside him dragging the sadly grounded kite back up the slope. Some part of him was still soaring yet another part was buried deep in the ground, lungs struggling for air, his eyes filled with earth. Louche sat beside him and watched through half-open eyes the sorry winding in of the tangled string. His father whispered into his ear, the words laboured, tense.

"You could maybe try a little harder, son."

THERE WAS A PEEP SHOW IN ANOTHER ARCH. Here there were more people than Louche had seen all night. They were two or three deep in front of the cage, which had been draped in black cloth. Around ten or so slits had been torn in the fabric, and the viewers, some with their hands on someone else, watched the participants of the peep show. There was both a sense of concentration and strange distraction as these bodies pressed against each other. Louche joined the viewers. Of course, inside his head a voice gushing with enthusiasm was veering from one suggestion to another—that he should be on the other side of the cage, that he should be running wild and feverish, that he could have been dipping and sucking and entwined, sublime amongst the assorted bodies splayed out in every stage of coitus. He worked his way to the front of the cage and shut his eyes letting the thin wire of the cage press into his face, gently then forcefully. Then, another voice rose inside him.

What are you doing here if you are not doing here.

Louche sank to his knees, and immediately people behind craned over him to view the orgy inside the cage. He felt a leg at his back, an elbow on his shoulder but these were accidental not intimate touches. When he opened his eyes there was only blackness and the relief that not being able to see brought to him. From open to shut there was no difference. That made sense to him, but again the hopeful voice in his head came back to him, forced open his eyes like rusty hinges and made his hands tore at the black material in front of him. A small gap opened and his eyelashes brushed the hairs on a man's arms which were pressing against the cage. Contact. His wildest dreams had never been this abstracted. His wildest dreams had him on the other side of the cage, his rubber shorts just another skin in a pile of limbs. His wildest dreams had brought him to this club of freedom, to set him free, to silence the undiminished voice in his head.

What are you waiting for, this is your chance…?

The arm moved away from the cage, to be replaced by the smooth skin of a woman's thigh that suddenly buffeted the side of the cage, a rhythm growing ever more insistent. He tore more of the fabric away and more was revealed.

He was so close he could smell something so personal that he scarcely believe it, he could see more than he had ever seen before. Louche put his hands down to his rubber shorts but his body felt numb, his nerves and senses blunted by the stimulation all around him until finally the persistent voice in his head reminded him what he already felt, already knew.

You are cold, cold, cold...

THE CONDUCTOR'S EYES WERE CLOSED. His head rocked forward then shook vigorously for a moment before jerking back, his wild hair falling around him. His shoulders were hunched but his arms raged around him, tentacles seemingly out of control then suddenly taut, suddenly loose. Louche turned to look at his father sitting beside him. His eyes too were closed, one hand brushing his eyelids while the other rested on the seat in front, his fingertips intermittently tapping the red velour. Through his own half-open eyes, Louche could see other people in the audience in a similar state to his father, all of them reacting to the music as it raged towards a crescendo, the drums thundering through his seat.

At a quiet moment, his father whispered into his ear.

"Marvellous, isn't it?"

He took his hand away from his face momentarily to squeeze Louche's hand.

And it was marvellous, Louche believed what he was told. His first concert, his first experience of live music, it was an evening of firsts. He should be proud. He was the only child in an audience of adults. There was something special about his presence there and yet his eyes remained only half-open, his vision squeezed into a loose line of blurred colour and unfocused bodies. He wanted to rock his head like the conductor, he wanted to run his hands along the harp, back and forward, laughing as the notes slid upwards. He wanted to run on to the stage and leap on to the cymbals crashing his way through the music. But a voice in his head offered no encouragement, teasing him only with the possibility of public humiliation.

How terrible it would to be suddenly on that stage and expected to play... He drew his body closer in, hugging his arms and legs, gathering his limbs tight against his chest. He needed to go to the toilet, he needed to clench his fists and stretch his legs so taut they would break and then there would be relief, a wash of wonderful warmth spreading over him and he could shut his eyes without thinking they should be open, he could let his voice out without fear of it being heard. He would not have to try anymore.

THE STREET OF SHAME, A CENTRAL CORRIDOR OF THE CLUB, was littered with couples in various states of sex. The light from the candles placed at even intervals along the narrow arch was surprisingly still, with little flicker to move or animate the bodies stretched out on the cobbled, uneven floors. Louche walked through these bodies with stealth, there still remaining a sense of expectation, a desire for invitation. Ahead of him, he saw another man, similar age, similar synthetic look, stop at one couple engaged in the early stages of arousal and kneel by them, outstretching a hand to the man's head and reaching down with his head to the woman's bare chest. Their arms welcomed him and drew him into their embrace. Louche smiled. This was what the evening was about. Encounters with strangers, exchanges of brief passion without guilt or long term attachment, a sense of revolution and sexual freedom. He'd been told it was an ideal way to explore yourself and lose inhibition about sex and intimacy. His optimistic voice, that hopeful half of him, reminded Louche to retain the smile to shore it up, fix it and anchor it in the face of doubt but even in the shadowy light of candles it was clear to see there was little humour creasing his thin lips.

Don't you wish that was you? Why can't it be you?

The warring voices in his head were the only thing Louche could hear at that moment. Yes, there was music, the sound of boots on cobbles, the grunts and groans of sex all around him but he was both deafened and muted by his own rage, clamouring for him to join in. Or not. He found another dark corner and pressed his bare back and legs against the cold brick. Now he was invisible, a white stain on the wall. He tried to stop all sound within him, to tighten it, strangle the words which kept coming back, on and on until his own breath stopped. Silence, somehow.

ALL THEY COULD HEAR WAS RAIN. The tent had begun to be weighed down by the torrential pour which had lasted more than three hours, just after the sun had set hurriedly at the end of the field. Louche could understand why. The enjoyment of the day had gone with the sun, the light drops of rain coming on as dusk shrouded them. It seemed to Louche that, with the sun gone, the clouds had rolled down from the hills surrounding them, rushing to coral them in their tents, one for the children, one for the adults. His cousins were enjoying themselves. They shed their given skins and let their naked limbs loose, a burst of energy, a smell of earth, sweat and something else. While in the adults' tent maybe ten metres away he could hear the clink of glasses, the low murmur of conversation; inside the children's tent there was a worm out of control, tunnelling its way in and out of the sleeping bags as the other cousin tried to kill it with one of the plastic picnic forks. Out of his squinting eyes, he could see the worm get closer to him but rather than watch the small figure burrowing towards him he watched the fork in the other boy's hand, raised and poised to strike.

I need to be somewhere else.

Soon the torchlight began to dim and he felt able to open his eyes. His cousins smothered the light under the material of the sleeping bag and the bright red glow became eyes in the gloom of the tent, their still playful bodies the tentacles of a serpent, the rain outside, was the hiss and spit of its hunger. Louche was so lost to the sensations around him he could barely talk, though when they spoke to him he replied, he told them his favourite games, his best sport, he reeled off the expected litany of likes and dislikes, but whether they knew it or not he was simply going through his paces. An expected recitation. The inevitable rituals. With raucous pageantry they showed him theirs while he hid from his, the palms of his hands pressed together, glued between his thighs.

He waited for the torches to die, their batteries to deaden, until they were unable to ignite the darkness with their penetrating beams. When at last they were plunged into darkness Louche began to emit low noises, part animal, part machine that came from the back of his throat, maybe from somewhere deeper. They hung in the air with menace. His cousins stopped talking and giggled at first and called him names, half surprised, half impressed. But when Louche continued to vocalise these sounds they asked him to stop, they wanted to sleep, they didn't know why he was making the sounds anymore. It wasn't funny. But he thought it was. Simply, naively funny.

After ten minutes Louche's father poked his head into the tent and told them to be quiet. He addressed himself to the cousins and not to Louche and this case of mistaken identity quietened him more than his father's gentle chastisement. While his cousins went to sleep he lay on his back, unable to curl up as they did, unable to get foetal as they did, unable to soften his grip on consciousness as they did. He lay awake all night, the sounds in his throat thwarted and held.

NEAR THE END OF THE NIGHT, Louche made it to the last arch, a narrow corridor hung with black drapes instead of candles, it was lanterns held on metal poles which splashed tight, yellow spots onto the ground The sound of his footsteps, the throb of music faded until all he could hear was the snarl of a whip.

He had expected to find more people in the arch. Everywhere he had gone that night there had been a throng of people, their desire and urgency, their lust and lingering desperation, being the brightest of lights a beam that penetrated his half-closed eyes.

A sign read, 'The Dungeon' and an attempt had been made to recreate some mediaeval sense of torture. Whips of differing lengths and widths were racked on to the wall as were restraints and other devices, their function uncertain to his inexperienced glance. The lash of the whip had not been a performance to a large crowd but the action of one solitary, hooded man. A strangely angular man who stood in front of one of the walls raising the whip and then bringing it down, sending the dust from the loose bricks flying in clouds around him.

Turn back, turn back, this isn't for you.

Now or never Louche, now or never.

The voices in his head were of course dominating everything, their ceaseless tussle reverberating as much as the sound of the whip in the empty arch but he swallowed hard and tried to take the voices with it, tried to take the voices and bury them somewhere deep and inaccessible. He didn't want to listen to them anymore and left alone he would have inevitably heard their insistence; left with no other distraction he might have surrendered and walked back along the gravel trail. The hooded man stopped mid-strike and through the black cloth Louche could see him squinting in the light of the lanterns his eyes meeting his. He quickly looked away but just as his gaze suddenly found a missing brick in the wall his hand was taken and led towards it. The same hand was raised into one of the shackles; attached to the wall; joined quickly by the other.

One, just one voice, like a deep and unwelcome sigh, surfaced quickly.

Is this what you want?

For once the question was left unanswered in the air, swirling incoherently with the clouds of brick dust. Without a word the hooded man stepped back, and Louche heard the whip trail along the floor. He was close to the wall, close enough for him to lick the dust from between the bricks, close enough for him to smell the dampness. He opened his eyes, fully, taking in all the available light, taking in everything within the limited scope. It seemed the richest of views. He waited for the persistent voice to say something, to make him balk and doubt his actions, but he heard nothing. The silence brought forward a surge of emotion, of tears and anger and laughter, rolling and gathering pace with each passing second.

Somewhere he heard his father sing BRING IT ON BRING IT ON BRING IT ON.

Somewhere he saw a young Louche hanging onto the kite that disappeared into the clouds.

Maria L. M. Fres-Felix

Collateral Damage

SHE PEPPERS HER LECTURES WITH THE STATEMENT, "As Professor Samuelson said…" in a tone implying that the Nobel laureate had confided in her some secret of the universe. In fact, she took *one* subject under Samuelson when she was sent to M.I.T. on a university scholarship in 1975. There, amid the rosy-gold foliage of a New England autumn, she marveled at the man who needed only one name to identify himself. Paul A. Samuelson, PhD, was superfluous. Just say Samuelson and people knew you were talking about the most influential post war economist alive. It was like being Einstein without the bad hair, or Cher, with brains.

Back here in Manila, and almost choking on jeepney fumes, she teaches Economics with the fervor of a true disciple of Economic Analysis.

"The law of supply and demand…" she would say, hands in her pockets, ever alert for some sign of life from her slack-faced students. As she paced, they would stare blankly at her hefty regal form, erect even at fifty-five, wrinkles spilling symmetrically on both sides of her round face like neatly drawn line graphs.

Sometimes, if she is lucky, someone would actually listen and think she is talking about a law passed in Congress, and then ask about applicable penalties. Those times, she would take a calming breath, flaring nostrils threatening to suck in the offender. Those times, she asks herself why she's such a sucker for heartache. Why she dutifully goes back year after year for more of the same indifference. Why she turned her back on more lucrative offers from the corporate world that could have taken care of her liposuction, dermabrasion, rhinoplasty, blapheroplasty, the whole caboodle, maybe even buy herself a boytoy. Each time, she is as clueless as the last.

So every given school day, she heaves her ample frame up the stairs and enters a classroom, a determined smile on her face. Her eyebrows knot when she sees some students all but necking. The tall hairy guy at the back is nuzzling that giggly girl perennially in shorts, like she is a cocktail appetizer. She surveys her class with the steely eyes of a drill sergeant while the overhead fan spews warm air over the classroom. She clears her throat, signaling the start of "Basic Economics."

She likes explaining things with graphs, deriving perverse pleasure from the grating squeal of chalk against blackboard. She draws "Figure 1: The Production Possibility Frontier" from memory. After all, she didn't get an "A" from Samuelson for nothing. She smiles at the twenty-eight-year-old memory.

FIG. 1. PRODUCTION POSSIBILITY FRONTIER

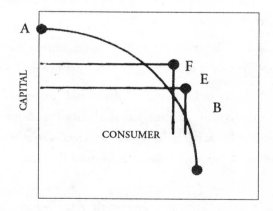

"The opportunity cost of producing more capital goods is fewer consumer goods," she explains. She calls on the tall hairy guy to give an example.

He stands up, lanky and self-assured, saying that the possibilities for self-improvement are endless, and that the consumer is king. He says such mindless things in perfectly accented English, not once blinking his dark eyes. He has such a perfect smile, all sixteen teeth bared in their immaculate whiteness, that she knows he has a bright future in politics, or show business, at least. *If,* he passes "Basic Economics." Better to flunk him and save the country some future trouble. Or does it matter?

Still, she thinks, perhaps it is her fault. The graph looks like a pregnant belly in profile. Maybe the concept can be better explained by saying, *"The opportunity cost of having a ballooning stomach, heavy with pregnancy is a reduced chance of graduating and hiding your shame."* Her gaze wanders to the giggly girl, who is staring at the tall guy, her large eyes sticky with adoration.

She feels her head throb, so she calls on a diligent student, the bespectacled boy who reminds her of a young, brown Samuelson. Sporting neatly combed hair, he is such a welcome contrast to all those other boys armed with greasy spikes for hair. Why, the guy even has his own pointer! Eagerly, he goes to the board, tracing the path of the Demand Curve, with reverence.

Fig. 2. Demand Curve

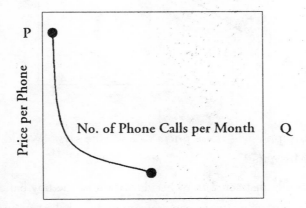

Samuelson look-alike says, "Demand curves have a negative slope, indicating that lower prices "P" cause quantity demanded "Q" to increase."

She could not have said it any better. There was hope, after all. But she catches herself thinking, *the more demands on a mother whose teenaged daughter gets pregnant, the more slumped her posture becomes, like the negatively sloping demand curve, till she turns into a shadow of her former self and just sits by the window, shoulders hunched, not minding how many good china the maids break, how the overseasoned adobo could send everybody to premature dialysis, how bad the grades of the two other daughters had become, or how frequently the husband passes out crossed-eyed drunk.*

Sometimes, when she is discussing "Supply," she is more hopeful. It is an easier concept, one even MTV-addled brains can handle.

FIG. 3. EXCESS SUPPLY OR SURPLUS

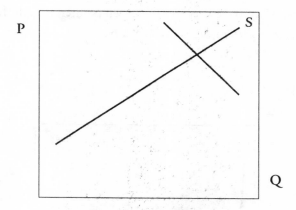

"Excess supply will cause prices to fall," she says. "Would you care to elaborate, Miss Yang?"

Temporarily distracted from her daydream of the boy band F4, Lenny Yang stands, butterfly tattoo peeping from under a baby tee, and says, "Oh, supplies, its when you don't know something's going to happen. Like a supplies party." With a grin, she throws both arms up in the air and says, "SUPPLIES!" like those bimbos who pop out of fake cakes.

The class laughs.

Smartass, she thinks, wanting with all her might to strangle Yang with the cord of the girl's Discman. But she lets it slide. Let's see who's going to get "suppliesed" by her grade at the end of the term, she says to herself. Grieve, even. Funny how the graph looks like a tombstone cross.

Excessive grief will cause the spirit to fall. An excess of sleeping pills will cause both spirit and body to fall. Shirley, her sister who couldn't even vote, elected to end her life. Sometimes, she wonders if it was the incessant crying of the baby, the days and nights cooped up at home when her friends were out dating, making the rounds of discos. Was it the constant hiding from neighbors and relatives? Was it the hopelessness? Or was it because of something Ruth did, or didn't do?

Nineteen sixty was not a good year to be 16, pregnant and unmarried in predominantly Catholic Philippines. Sure, they already watched picture shows in their living room through the marvel of television, but it would take three decades at least before unmarried starlets and bold stars would breezily claim on national TV that God was with them when they "did it," and then affect an air of righteousness and martyrdom for deciding against abortion.

She takes a chalk and draws another graph.

FIG. 4. PERFECTLY ELASTIC DEMAND

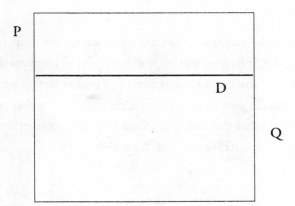

From memory, she says, "Quantity demanded is fixed. A tiny price increase drives the quantity demanded to zero."

A hand shoots up, and she gratefully calls on an unfamiliar-looking student of indeterminate gender. She does not know if the confusion lies in the wild, rust-colored hair, loose pants and shirt, or the assortment of body rings. She does not even know if the student is a member of her class. Well, anything for a distraction.

The student says in a voice that is too low for a girl's but a bit high for a boy's, "Ma'am, what about shabu? Even if the price increases, the demand remains high. You know, maybe shabu and other drugs can stimulate the economy."

A handful of students hoot. The androgyne smirks.

"Settle down," she says in a tone of dismissive scorn. Her right hand is thrust deep in her pocket, her arm growing more rigid by the second. "It is precisely because the demand for such substance is not fixed. Neither is it legal." She reassembles her face into an expression of calm that she does not feel. Meanwhile, she is thinking of a thousand and one ways to torture this budding felon, calculating how long it will take till the androgyne's heartbeat flatlined like the graph. Oh, how much it looked like her father's heart monitor.

Expectations are fixed. Chastity was one, regard for life, another. Shirley was his favorite. Didn't he give her extra allowance when she ran out? Didn't he let her "steal" the car once in a while? Perhaps her father's heart could not take it anymore and flatlined.

Trying as these lessons are, they are no match for the more intricate ones on business cycles, inflation, and employment. Not to mention the multiplier effect. How can she cut through their hormonal haze and make them understand that the output changes by a multiple of the change in planned investments? And that this multiple is called the multiplier effect? She herself sometimes gets quantitative overload from these.

For classes on those topics, she takes breathing spells: breathing in through the nose, holding the breath for a count of eight, then exhaling through the mouth. Sometimes, she just takes a Prozac.

Fig. 5. The Business Cycle

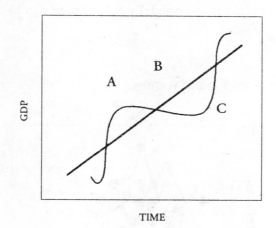

TIME

"When the economy moves from a peak (A) down to a trough (C), through point B, the economy is in recession." She surveys her work on the board, making sure that the points are precise. The periodic ups and downs remind her of her binges.

When she feasts and fasts, her weight fluctuates like a roller coaster. Her mood swings from frustration to depression. She keeps wondering why her mother never put her on a slimming diet like she did with her older sister Shirley, or bring her to the dermatologist when acne ravaged her face like a rampaging army of termites. Sometimes, she blames her mother for her failure to get married.

She thinks she started overeating because her parents had not believed her when she told them what Shirley did with her boyfriend whenever only the three of them were in the house. She remembers how she threw up when, as a grown-up, she realized what they had been doing.

She looks at her students in slinky tops, and feels a tinge of envy. Then she notices how they seem to cling koala-like to their boyfriends, and she feels a sense of loss and foreboding. Sometimes she wants to shake them out of their stupor. You came to school to study, and not live from climax to climax. Certainly not to have an unwanted pregnancy.

She draws the graph with a hint of savagery, the chalk screeching in agony. The kinks are quite pronounced and sharp. She steadies her hand as she drops the chalk into the bin.

FIG. 6. UNEMPLOYMENT AND INFLATION

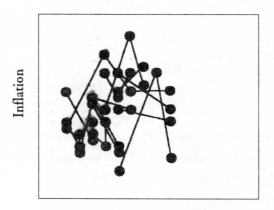

Unemployment Rate

On autopilot, she drones on, "During the 1970s, and the 1980s, it became clear that the relationship between unemployment and inflation was anything but simple."

Just like the relationship between Shirley's pregnancy and Ruth's sanity. Or like the tormented waves in Ruth's brain.

Sometimes, Ruth, the youngest, recognizes them. The nurses say she hums a lullaby all the time. Perhaps the same lullaby she used to sing to Shirley's baby. Or perhaps the snappy rhyme she recited when she tossed the baby like a ball, high, then higher still in the air. Happily mouthing the words and giggling, till she failed to catch the baby and the giggle died in her throat, just as the baby gurgled with finality.

Her father's connections made the death officially SIDS. Everybody was just too willing to help Shirley. She had gone through so much, and her young life was all but ruined. If only they knew the extent of collateral damage. Ruth, her father, her mother, and herself. She had to raise herself and take care of her mother and Ruth. Did they know that? If they did, maybe they'd stop gossiping.

Or gossip even more.

There is a strange sound in her ears, and it is not her raspy breathing. With the back of a pudgy hand she wipes the perspiration crawling down her forehead. Breathe deeply, she prods herself.

The teenage felon is saying something and the rest of the class is snickering. "Ma'am, I said, so what did the great Samuelson have to say to that problem of inflation and unemployment?"

She has difficulty breathing. If only she had taken her Prozac.

"I mean, if he's so good, why hasn't he figured it out?"

Their faces are no longer slack, but contorted with glee. Or is it triumph about having saved all their pranks and wisecracks especially for her? She looks at the tall guy, arm draped around the giggly girl, who could be pregnant and not know it. She looks at the horny faces of the other disasters-in-waiting, then back at the hectoring teen-age felon. She stiffens. She sees nothing but ruined lives inexorably ruining others in turn. The multiplier effect.

She fingers the pearl-handled snub-nosed beauty inside her pocket. It could be so easy, she tells herself. Then a glint of spectacles catches her eyes, and she is staring into the earnest visage of the diligent Samuelson look-alike. Her nostrils quiver as she sighs, fingers slowly uncurling.

Maybe another day.

✦

ZOË STRACHAN

After they'd gone

AFTER THEY HAD GONE, THEY BECAME A KIND OF URBAN MYTH, helped by the fact that Hazel had written a song about them. It wasn't quite Terry and Julie in Waterloo Station, but as the band became more popular, people who knew the song and lived in the area might occasionally say:

"There's the street Sylvie lived in!" or, "That's where Jack and Sylvie met."

Like anyone who had ever known Jack and Sylvie together, as a couple, Hazel could picture them clearly. Individually they were fairly good-looking, not absolutely stunning, but more attractive than most. Put together though, they were suddenly striking. It was to do with attitude; together they behaved differently, were more quietly confident, more poised. The whole seemed greater than the sum of its two halves. Having said that, it helped that they looked a bit like Bob Dylan and Joan Baez, although to be fair, Jack was prettier and wore better clothes than Bob. The clothes were important. Jack and Sylvie always managed to give the impression that they'd made no effort, while looking as if they'd been carefully styled for a retro fashion feature.

The other thing which people tended to remember about Jack and Sylvie was the mermaid. Hazel had heard about the mermaid from Jack. Not long after that she bumped into Sylvie in the street and went to her flat for a cup of tea. While the kettle was boiling, Sylvie took Hazel into the bedroom to introduce her. The mermaid didn't have a name, Sylvie just called her 'the mermaid.' She was dark-skinned and shiny, with long glossy hair which fell in waves and swirls around her breasts. She was quite obviously a mermaid, because just below her delicate little navel her smooth skin changed to scales. Unfortunately she had lost most of her tail when she was broken off the prow of her ship. Even so, she was almost as tall as Hazel.

"Let's have our tea through here, she likes company," Sylvie said, and went back to the kitchen to fetch it. Hazel perched on the edge of the bed, honoured to meet the mermaid but awkward at being left alone with her. She almost felt as though she should be making conversation. The mermaid had properly carved eyes, she noticed, not the blank spaces some statues had. Sylvie came back in with a teapot, cups and biscuits on a tray. Hazel half expected to see three cups instead of two.

"She's lovely Sylvie. Where did you get her?"

Sylvie stirred her tea, took a sip.

"Well, I was in Orkney, just for some time to myself. A few years ago now. I went to see Scara Brae, then I walked along the beach at Skaill Bay. It was empty, and quiet except for the wind in my ears and the waves lapping at the sand. I looked for shells, then went down to the water's edge and watched the sea swelling. I saw something dark bobbing about in the grey water, but it took me a while to figure out what it was. When I realised, I took off my shoes and coat and waded in. It was freezing, and she was further away than I thought. I had to go in up to my armpits to reach her, and I was frightened I'd be swept away. But I struggled against the sea and pulled her safely to shore."

"That's amazing."

"That was only the beginning. I had to drag her over the sand dunes and up to the road, hitch a lift back to Stromness and my B&B. Everyone thought I was mad. I thought I'd got pneumonia. I shivered and sneezed for days, but it was worth it."

She patted the mermaid's side affectionately.

"Of course, Orcadian legend has it that if you find a mermaid, you're responsible for her forever. Whatever you do, she'll never let you go. Not that I'd be without her."

That was the only time Hazel met the mermaid, but the memory stayed with her. It was like a gift, to balance Sylvie falling in love with her best friend, taking him away. And so, eventually, Hazel wrote the song. She started with the evening Jack and Sylvie got together. It became the first verse. They met at a northern soul night at the RAFA club. A mutual acquaintance, drunkenly ensuring everyone knew everyone else, introduced them. To be honest they would probably have ended up with each other anyway. As it was, they couldn't believe they had never met before. They talked together, danced together, went back to Sylvie's together and, in the end, slept together.

When Jack thought back to that night, it wasn't having sex with Sylvie which he particularly remembered, although that had certainly been a highlight. No, it was meeting the mermaid for the first time which really stuck in his mind. It seemed to him that even while they were in bed, he kept finding himself looking over Sylvie's shoulder to the mermaid in the corner. He could recall her lips, her eyes, her expression.

Hazel gently edited the story, captured it in lines and rhythms. When she sang the song her mind filled it out, added pictures, remembered meeting Jack and Sylvie in a café the next day, holding hands over the table.

A while later, in the same café but at a different table, Hazel, Jack and a girl called Pearl were having coffee. The mermaid came up in conversation. Hazel said, "It's such a beautiful story, isn't it? How Sylvie found her, I mean."

Jack laughed, "Depends whether you think rooting about in skips is beautiful!"

Puzzled, Hazel said, "But it was in Orkney, wasn't it? Sylvie rescued her from the sea."

"No," Jack said, "It was in Otago Street. God knows where she came from, or who was throwing her out."

Hazel was about to argue but Pearl got in first, "Sylvie said the mermaid was a family heirloom. It came from the wreck of a pirate ship originally. Her great great grandfather brought it back from the West Indies last century."

Jack was worried. Had Sylvie lied to him? He couldn't imagine that, didn't want to. Or had she just made up more romantic stories for everyone else? And if she had lied to him, why hadn't she gone to more trouble, invented a special lie? She had crafted a whole myth for Hazel. Unless that really was the truth. He turned it over and over in his mind.

That night, as usual, Jack went round to Sylvie's flat. They sat in her room, listening to music and chatting. Sylvie opened some wine and lit some candles. Finally Jack asked her where she'd got the mermaid.

"I told you," Sylvie said. "I bought her in a junk shop in Edinburgh."

"No, you told me you found her in a skip in Otago Street."

"Oh, did I?"

Sylvie seemed unconcerned. She poured herself another glass of wine. Jack hadn't expected this reaction and wasn't sure how to proceed. He looked at the mermaid, who was gleaming in the candlelight. It made her hair look shinier than usual, in fact it looked almost like real hair, as if it would be soft to touch. Jack turned to Sylvie and tried again,

"You told Hazel a story about pulling her out the sea beside Scara Brae."

Sylvie remained non-committal.

"And you told Pearl that she was an heirloom."

They were about to have their first argument about the mermaid. Sylvie insisted it didn't matter where the mermaid came from, and if she wanted to tell different people different stories then that was her business. Jack didn't understand why she wouldn't tell him the truth. He could keep it secret if she wanted. In the end, Sylvie sent him away, and off he went, angry and still none the wiser.

But the next day they made up, and as a peace offering Sylvie let him help her polish the mermaid. She brought out a tin of lavender-scented wax and some chamois cloths.

"Okay," Jack said. "Where will I start?"

"Well, I like doing her hair best, so I'll start at her head. You can begin at her scales and work your way up."

Sylvie sang wordlessly to herself as she coated her chamois with polish and started smoothing it on to the mermaid's hair and face. Jack watched her for a second before he began. It looked as if Sylvie were putting conditioner on the mermaid's hair, strand by strand, applying makeup to her skin. She didn't just rub the wax all over, instead she carefully blended it on to the mermaid's eyelids, cheekbones, lips, pausing to check the effect as she polished it up to a sheen. Jack realised that this was a ritual, and had to be performed with a suitable amount of ceremony.

He did the scales around the mermaid's hips more or less individually, then sat back and considered her stomach and waist. The smell of the polish was strong, like incense. Warm and floral and musky all at once. He rubbed his chamois against the pale lilac balm, smeared it over the wood until it turned creamy and opaque. Then he started massaging the polish in, scooping some excess from her navel with his pinky. Meanwhile, Sylvie was working on the mermaid's arms, which were held up, her hands clasped behind her head, buried under her hair.

Jack followed the grain, buffing the wood until it shone, acutely conscious of the shape of the mermaid's body. He had always liked her, from the very first moment he had seen her, but he had never been this close, not until now. He felt how her tummy curved outwards while the small of her back arched in, noticed how full her hips were, the scales starting at their widest point, how she swept inwards at the waist. She had what was called an hourglass figure, he supposed, as he skimmed her sides with his chamois. Sylvie spotted him slowing.

"Put some elbow grease into it! You'll never see your reflection like that."

Jack renewed his efforts, trying to concentrate on the polishing, rubbing harder and harder. When he rested one hand on the mermaid for support, the wood felt warm with all the attention it had been given. Like real skin, if skin was ever that sleek or flesh ever that firm. He gave her tummy a final wipe and admired his handiwork. Sylvie was still polishing the mermaid's hair where it flowed in front of her shoulders.

"Nearly finished. We can do one breast each if you like?"

"Okay," Jack agreed, picking up his cloth again. The mermaid had a very impressive bosom, and both her nipples were clearly visible, carefully carved. Jack began to polish her right breast, avoiding the couple of curls of hair spiralling over it. As he followed the curve with his hand, Jack became aware of something that he hadn't expected. He felt kind of ridiculous; all he was doing was polishing a bit of wood after all. But as his arousal grew so did his knowledge that the mermaid wasn't just carved wood.

He sat on the bed watching Sylvie finish her half. She seemed quite happy, but her actions were more clinical, like a nurse giving a patient a bed bath. At last she folded up her cloth and sat down next to Jack. They both looked at the shining mermaid. Sylvie started to say something, but Jack pulled her towards him and kissed her.

A little later, lying in bed, Jack found himself comparing Sylvie to the mermaid. Sylvie's hair was poker straight, the mermaid's wavy. Her skin was pale and matte, the mermaid's glowed. Sylvie had a slim, boyish figure, the mermaid was strong and voluptuous. He tried to stop thinking that way but he couldn't get the mermaid out his mind. He didn't open his eyes because he knew she would be standing there, looking at him, smiling at him.

"Sylvie?"

"Mmmhmm?"

Jack kept his tone casual.

"Where did the mermaid come from?"

Sylvie chuckled.

"Before I met you, a year or two before, I was going out with this boy, John, who was in his final year at art school."

"Uh-huh?"

"He was studying sculpture. He carved her for his degree show. Got a distinction. Then he gave her to me as a present. I didn't want to tell you before in case you were jealous."

Jack didn't really believe Sylvie. She got up, saying she was going to have a bath, and when she was safely gone he got out of bed and went over to the mermaid.

Hazel could imagine all this vividly. She could picture Jack standing entranced, gazing at the mermaid as she gleamed softly in the darkness, not so much enticing as provocative, full of abandon. Jack was taller than her. He had to stoop to breathe in her scent. She hadn't been carved by an art student, he knew. He could smell the sea from her, mingled with the faded aroma of lavender. His hand looked very white against her dark locks as he traced their waves and curls with his fingertips. Feeling daring, he brushed her cheek with his lips. He almost expected her to move, but of course she didn't, she stayed absolutely still and passive. Gaining confidence, he ran his hands down her sides, stroking the curve of her waist and hips, stopping when his palms reached her scales. He kissed her mouth this time. She had very full, pouty lips, slightly parted so he could just stick the tip of his tongue between them. She tasted of salt, like sea water or sweat.

Sylvie walked into the room while Jack was caressing the mermaid. He didn't hear her bare feet on the carpet, didn't stop what he was doing. She saw him kneeling, naked, to kiss the mermaid's stomach. Watched him run his tongue up between her breasts, press his lips to her nipples. All that ran through Sylvie's mind was how? How can she, how will he? Jack stood up, wrapped his arms around the mermaid and Sylvie couldn't watch any more, couldn't speak, couldn't bear to let him know she was there. The mermaid seemed to be looking at her, rather than at Jack. Sylvie crept back through to the bathroom, locked the door, and sank into the warm water.

While she was onstage, singing, Hazel often felt nervous. When she sang the song about Jack and Sylvie and the mermaid however, she became quite unaware of the audience. The thought of Sylvie tiptoeing away to cry in the bath could make her own eyes water. And Hazel still missed them. It wasn't long after that night that Jack and Sylvie went away.

They didn't really talk about it, and after they had gone people never quite remembered where they'd moved to, except that it was an island. Nobody got a letter, and only Hazel received an abrupt, battered postcard: "We did it." Jack and Sylvie had decided to make a clean break. They loaded everything they wanted to keep into Jack's rickety old car. Sylvie wrapped the mermaid in a white cotton sheet and she and Jack carried her downstairs and laid her gently along the back seat of the car. Hazel slipped her hand under the sheet to touch the mermaid's head for the last time, surreptitiously ran her thumb over those carved wooden eyes. Then she waved goodbye to Jack and Sylvie as they drove off. She remembered it had been a bright, sunny afternoon.

They had chosen a nighttime ferry crossing to the island, one that would be quiet. As planned, they waited for the sleepiest, most silent moment. After checking that nobody was about, they carried the mermaid up onto the deck. Jack steadied her while Sylvie slipped the sheet off and the three of them stood for a second, looking out over the water. Jack and Sylvie exchanged glances. Without speaking, they each kissed the mermaid on the cheek, then lifted her up and pushed her over the railing so that she dived head first into the sea and disappeared beneath the waves.

That was to be the end of the song, but a coda insinuated itself in Hazel's mind and would not leave. It is as clear an image to her as that of Jack and Sylvie walking hand in hand, or Sylvie dragging the mermaid onto a sandy shore. In the final verse, Jack and Sylvie lie sleeping in a room Hazel does not recognise. Jack is still, but Sylvie is agitated, tossing from side to side, her dark hair tangling over the pillow. She is dreaming of the sea again, Hazel knows, of water which should feel cold as it sprays up against her naked body. Saltwater tears are streaming out from under her closed and trembling eyelashes.

Angelo R. Lacuesta

Survivors

THEY ALL THOUGHT Fishman had gills. He always wore a black rubber swimming cap, tight against his skull, over the tops of his ears. He had the gills there, they said, right behind his ears. He'd stay down more than anyone ever could. Someone said he once stayed down for ten minutes, fixing a tangled net.

Everyone wanted him. The boat captains would call out to him when they saw him, hiring him for the next ride out. Sometimes he'd say yes, and show up right before the boat pushed from dock. Sometimes he's say no, because he'd been booked a full month. Sometimes he'd be booked for a full month.

I dunked the plastic pitcher into the salt water and poured it out into the glass. In the moonlight it looked just as cloudy as the gin mix anyway. They'd wake up the next morning shitting out their guts and wondering why they had a salty taste in their mouth. I'd never had the nerve to tell them why, but once or twice I almost did. What stopped me was Fishman, who I'm sure knew it as soon as he brought the thick glass to his mouth, the taste of seawater, clear and undiluted to his lips even after whole bottles of gin. And he drank it anyway, like it was the best gin-pomelo he'd ever tasted. If it were gin he'd probably be out cold, anyway. But the next morning he'd be up way before anybody else was, checking the lines, cleaning the nets.

He'd just look at me, smirking. The seawater was nothing to him. The sea was nothing to him, either.

The fish-whore noticed it, too. His smell, like oily fish, like the seawater at low tide close to the shore, strewn with garbage. She recognized it instantly, I think, the smell of Fishman. After all, she'd probably been around here longer than any of us. I was the newest one here, a mechanic who was more used to V8 and V10 truck engines, then on a lark tried my hand at the recycled, reconditioned Mitsubishis and Fusos they had in fishing boats. The other guys, they were deadbeats, bums who had picked up the simple trade and learned it along the way. The captain, he was probably a deadbeat, too. It was morning of our second week. The ice had almost melted out down in the hold. It was just mostly cold water keeping the catch fresh—or mostly fresh. I doubted they'd pass off as fresh, even if the wholesalers saw us coming to dock and unloading them. They'd probably smell a bit off by then, too.

All we had was a lucky bounty from the third day of our trip, our only luck ever since. There was a good mound of them in the hold, squid and mackerel, half-covered in water.

She sat beside Fishman quietly while she waited for the captain, not looking at him. She had some beauty under her dry, brown skin, though I was far from an authority on that, especially then. I hadn't fucked a woman for a long time. Her husband waited in their pumpboat, its outrigger moored to our boat.

The captain had Tambo fill two pails with the fish. Mostly dead, except for a few twitching mackerel, wriggling their tails and gasping in the dirty water. They'd probably get a good profit from it at the market, considering it would be still relatively fresh. It was money without much hard work, too. Unless you counted her work—which was probably not much.

Two pails was worth one fuck for the captain. Probably thirty, forty-five minutes' worth. While they were at it in his quarters the husband waited in his boat, like it was safer there, like it was a security measure. He unloaded the fish into baskets, ready for the market. He read a comic book while he waited. The pumpboat bobbed up and down, knocking the outrigger against our hull, making it difficult to read.

"Know how to read?" I asked Fishman. He was looking at him, too, studying what he was doing. There was nothing else to look at.

"No," he said. They told me he'd been swimming as soon as he was born. That his mother ate nothing but tuna during her pregnancy. Maybe she was a fish-whore, too. I could believe that one.

You couldn't get hungry out here. But it's not just the sea. Everywhere. I told Fishman once about an uncle of mine. When I was a child he took me up the mountains near our town—I didn't even know what those mountains were called. It didn't make a difference, anyway. To me every forest, every mountain looked the same from the ground.

I never knew we were expecting to spend the night there until he took out a small plastic bag of rice grains for dinner. It was going to get dark soon and I realized we were staying here, in the middle of the mountain forest.

My uncle cut a two-foot segment from a bamboo stalk, with nodes on both ends so it formed a hollow container. It was thick around as his thigh. Then he used the pointed end of his itak to bore a small hole on the side. He formed a funnel out of banana leaf and poured the rice into it. Then he took water from a stream and funneled that in, too.

Over one shoulder he carried an air-rifle that he had fitted out so it would take .22 bullets. He fired at a couple of forest lizards and both turned belly up as soon as they were hit. I hadn't even seen the lizards until he shot them. When we went over to get them I couldn't even see where the bullets hit their thick hide. They weren't even wounded. My uncle told me that the shock of getting hit was enough to startle them, render them inert and unconscious. He taught me how to skin them and clean them. He chopped the lizards up and put them in a milk can he had brought along. There was stuff in it already, whole garlic and chopped onions. I also smelled pepper. He buried the milk can in the soil, gathered some sticks on it, and started a fire. Then, a bamboo tripod over the fire. He placed the rice cooker on the tripod.

While it was cooking he made a makeshift shelter with the rest of the bamboo stalks and with the largest leaves we could find. And then we sat and we waited.

"Reading must be a lot of fun," Fishman said, smirking.

A gust of wind blew fresh salt into the air. Fishman seemed to luxuriate in it. I saw his eyes close and his brow crumple, as though he was trying hard not to show me how good it felt to him. That oily smell again now, a bit darker and bolder than the smell of the fish that had spent a week in cold, dirty water, earlier passed to the fish-whore's husband.

Maybe he just didn't take baths. People had a smell, a unique, unmistakable smell. I know about this. I'd been living and sleeping among people since I can't remember. I'd never thought about how true that was until now. It was always among people, a common mattress on the floor with my parents, a bunk bed in a barracks, a rundown dormitory.

The man's wife had the smell of baby cologne and powder. It made me dizzy to think about where she had applied either. But now it was Fishman's smell again, as it inevitably became Fishman's smell everywhere: in the holds, in the containers, on the ropes. Even the fish smelled more of him than just fish. It was the smell of fish-man, a mix of maleness and supple oil, and like the sea, a faint odor of decay. He had a small, uncommonly sharp nose and small, swept-back eyes, and his rubber swimming cap was stretched and furrowed enough to resemble part of his skin, his head.

I suppose this made him look good-looking, too, and gave him a kind of sharpness of look and a temperamental, introspective frown. But while the fish-whores tried to work their charms on the rest of us—for a hundred bucks each instead of baskets of fish—they all seemed to pay special attention to him. Though I'd never seen him really interested in them. He preferred to stay downstairs in the hold, or, overboard on the other side of the boat, inside the sea, head piercing the surface from time to time.

The thing was, none of us had enough pesos to enjoy her more than once in a couple of months. She was walking out on the deck now, her appearance carefully resorted and some of the scent of powder replaced by sweat.

"Salamat, Manong," she said, to no-one in particular. Her step was a little looser now, her balance a bit off. She brushed against Fishman as she passed. She turned to look at him—was it the smell?—looked right at his face and smiled. She knew him.

Then it struck me that I would have been surprised if they didn't know each other; everyone knew the fish-whore was much, much older than she said she was; and simply everyone—in the boat business, in the town—knew Fishman. How many times could they have met? On this boat or any of the others that plied these parts?

He might have fucked her a couple of times, too.

"It's done."

I didn't know how my uncle knew things like that. I had known him enough at the time to know that it really was done, and that it was time to retrieve the bamboo rice cooker and to stamp out the fire and unearth the milk can. When both were opened, the bamboo split open, the milk can cover pried off, the smell caused a kind of triumphant pleasure between us.

Lizard tastes better than chicken. It's lean, dark and delicate so that eating the bones clean makes the flavor all the better. It's easy to capture and found in great numbers, so that people like my uncle and I could find ourselves complete and satisfied in the middle of the jungle.

He had told me he often found the urge to walk up the mountain like this and spend some nights alone. I shuddered at this, hating myself for being such a coward. He had told me our jungles had few predators and he had an anting-anting that protected him from common jungle animals and evil spirits. Besides, he understood its ways and knew how to handle its creatures.

He had told me once about the time he slept on a bed of banana leaves in the open. It was summer and there was no chance it would rain. He had been awakened, in the middle of the night, the full moon already high, to a strange breathing sound at his ear.

"O—take it easy, boss," he had said, half asleep. "I'm just passing through. I mean you no harm. Just a few lizards."

And he had drifted back to sleep afterward.

"So how many times have you fucked her?"

"Once or twice. Maybe more," he said, the answer quick and easy.

"I haven't even."

"Nothing to worry about."

Fishman was in charge of making sure the nets were OK down there. He could stitch the nets, make knots and unravel them under there, as fast and as sure as anyone could on land. He dislodged them from rocks and unruly corals. We were sure he could catch two pails of fish faster than the net could, considering it took some waiting and some luck.

It was just me and Fishman, now, the last bottle of gin between us, with no more lime juice, not even a single calamansi.

The rest of the crew had passed out drunk at an earlier hour. It was the captain's guilt at work. He knew he had deprived us of some earnings, considering we took a cut out of every load we brought in. To add to that, he also knew he had fucked a woman and none of us could afford to. He had the right to the catch. It was always thanks to the captain's luck and skill that led a boat to its quota. Everyone thought it was dignified enough of him, even in some small way.

They were all old hands of his, old friends. He was godfather to many of their children, and once or twice he would reward one or two of them with a round with one of the fish-whores, after him, of course.

But Fishman and I were outside this circle; he was a freelancer, and made too much money that way, and maybe because of that, very few friends. I was a truck mechanic on his first month at this job. And as with all my previous trades, I knew this one wouldn't last.

"It's because of you, of course," I told him.

He saw me looking at the boat's rear, where the dark hold heaped with quiet, silver fish, the once-iridescent lines on their sides faded away. Hanging above the hold, I could barely make out the dark, linked-diamond shapes of more fish, split, salted and hung from fishing lines to dry. The moon was not out yet.

Fishman merely grinned. He had heard this before, of course, just as I had: he had a smell for the sea, a sense of where to go; or, he was a lucky talisman to have on board, so that every boat that got him would be back at the dock earlier than scheduled, heavy with catch, and the captains would be standing there, waiting, because they all knew he was done and he would be looking for a new job.

I asked Fishman why he bothered to live this way. How much would it take to buy you a boat, second- or third-hand, with a good V10 engine. I could even help you get a cheap one and make sure you don't get cheated. I knew a little bit about construction and wood. I certainly knew my way with engines. It's the Fusos you want. Don't bother with the Mitsubishis or the Isuzus, no matter what they tell you. It's the salt water, you see. Fusos are built to last—the rest will die out on you. At least I've never had a Fuso give out on me.

And then a few thousand more to get you started out. A good brand new net, a good supply of ice in the hold, plus the little extras: a kerosene lamp, a kerosene cooker. A couple cases of gin. That would be a good month's worth.

"I don't have that kind of money," Fishman said, half listening. He was looking at the drying fish, glistening brighter now.

I didn't have to tell him that all the boats he worked on for two months would make more than that kind of money; they were making money off him, off his luck, his skill—I almost mentioned his gills. But I told him anyway.

Fishman looked young, but I was quite sure it was the sea that had smoothed out his skin and stretched it taut against his sharklike face.

"We're getting old, Fishman."

He stood up, bounded across the deck, his feet making two wet slaps against the boards, and disappeared soundlessly into the water. Before he got back on board I drifted into a sitting sleep.

When we ran out of rice, my uncle and I fell to scrounging for sweet potatoes. It was no difficult sacrifice. The lizards were always there, flashing their scales dimly at us as we sat in the twilight, and we had enough bullets in our pockets to keep us hunting for days.

My uncle died when he was in his early fifties. They found him in the forest, up a tree. It was the smell that led them there. He was lodged in a crotch of thick branches, as though he had perched his body there to make sure he wouldn't slip down to the ground even if he had fallen asleep.

They also saw fierce scratch-marks on the bark. Might have been warthogs or wild dogs. Some people suggested it was supernatural creatures. Prayers were offered and a chicken was slaughtered and offered to the jungle before they took him down. He'd been there days, probably. But he had tried his best. The tree had edible fruit, even if it was almost unbearably bitter and tough. He had his milk can with him, rattling as his corpse trundled to the ground. When they opened it they found lizard bones, eaten clean. But it still smelled of fresh garlic, onion and ginger.

"He was a survivor," they told me. A part of me knew he was, and I even clearly remember crying at the thought of him crouching in that tree. But a part of me knew he wasn't really a survivor. For one thing, if he were, he'd still be alive now.

We were on our way back now. There was a new mood in the air. The men began talking about what they were going to spend their pay on.

"Straight to Aling Taring, that bitch. That bitch has got a damn keen sense of smell. She knows whenever I've just come in."

"Well my bitch is named Alex. Alexandra. At the Catwalk Club. She probably got that name from an American movie. Her cunt's got that same sense of smell. She knows when I'm loaded and milks me dry."

When it was still freshly caught, we liked to eat it raw and squirming. But now it was dried fish for breakfast, dried fish for lunch and dried fish for dinner. Still, it tasted different here, the salt-taste cleaner and the flesh more tender. Fishman had taught us to like it half-broiled, still pink and bloody inside. Then he caught a basketful of squid and we rinsed the small slippery bodies in water, took a long knife and split them down the middle to take out the soft bone. Then we swirled them in vinegar before swallowing them, sticky and squirming.

There was no more gin, but captain took heart enough to bring out a bottle of brandy from his personal stash. He poured a bit into the vinegar and when we dipped the squid heads into it we had never tasted it this good. Then he poured some into the empty Nescafé diamond glass and passed it around.

My uncle always told me that brandy should be drunk slow and steady. Which was why it was for old people, rich people, people with experience, because they knew how to take pleasure from a long, slow session.

My boatmates, though, knocked each glass back. Either they didn't know how to drink it or they just missed the gin so much. It was a session even the captain couldn't last. I knew he didn't want to look weak to his men, that he could knock it back as fast as they could. Whenever my turn came I'd make sure my hand covered the glass so they couldn't see how little I'd poured.

Fishman drank like a fish. His red face stood out in stark contrast from his flesh-colored swim cap. He had a full glass, the last of the brandy, in his hand. I'd poured out the bottle until it was empty.

"Drink up, Fishman. There's nobody here left. Even your captain is down."

Fishman raised the glass to me and bottomed it out, the muscles on his neck flattening and thickening.

"Puta!" he said, slamming down the thick tumbler.

I asked him how he was going to spend his money.

"My wife."

"Never knew you had a wife. Got kids?"

"Two. Not from the same wife," he added, grinning.

I laughed. I imagined that this was how the captain would do it, laughing out loud at jokes that weren't really that funny. It was his way of keeping his men tight and keeping them together.

"My wife is not here, actually," he said.

I looked at him, wanting to show him I was listening. I knew the setup: wife working as a domestic helper in Singapore or Hong Kong or Saudi, the husband underqualified for any opening. Men would take the skilled jobs, the foremen jobs, the engineer jobs. They couldn't be maids. Nobody needed fishermen. Nobody needed mechanics either, unless they had college degrees and could pass those exams in English.

"If you had your own boat, you wouldn't need to pay to fuck. Think of how many pails of fish you'd be able to get. You could live forever out here. You wouldn't even have to go back to land."

Fishman was too drunk to dive by now. I could smell the smell of alcohol mixing with his oily smell. There was also the smell of fragrant smoke, of broiled fish, now reduced to a heap of white bones and fish-skulls on the plate between us. It reminded me of the smell of uncle's milk can.

"Look at them," I grunted, dipping my eyes half-closed the way men do when they are drunk. The men lay snoring on the deck, limbs askew, bellies exposed.

The moon had given us enough light. We worked in a kind of underwater silence. We tied them up tight with fishing line and stuffed their mouths with rags. Then we slit their throats with clean, sure strokes. We counted them all to make sure we had them all, and unloaded them one by one off the deck.

He covered his nose and mouth, like he was going to throw up. I imagined he could smell the blood from their bodies and on the deck. I told him to relax on the reardeck, by the hold, near the fish, while I filled a bucket with seawater so I could clean up.

"We're survivors," I told him.

A small wind picked up the smell of their blood, greasy and salt, with a sharp alcohol tinge. In the moonlight it looked like a fresh coating of paint.

ADRIAN SEARLE

The Magpie

THE BIRD WATCHED MICHAEL WITH A SINGLE BLACK EYE as its head flicked and clicked from side to side with the rigid geometry of a clockwork toy. Although the window was wide open, the smell inside the shed was stifling, heavy with the odour of compost and two-stroke engine oil. Stepping carefully between a large paper sack of seed potatoes and a collection of ancient but still lethal garden implements, Michael reached over and gave the cage a yank, dragging it a foot or so out from its hiding place. The bird flapped furiously for a few moments, disturbed by the motion, but then settled again, leaving a rising cloud of stour, ten thousand tiny filaments illuminated in the shafts of sunlight.

The magpie made scratching little hops in a small circle, its movements constrained by the wire prison. A long tapering tail poked out through the bars and, even though it seemed to him juvenile, Michael had the urge to reach out and touch the feathers, to feel the texture of the opalescent blackness as it pitter-pattered against the wires. The plumage was striking, like a zebra crossing or one of those Mary Quant dresses Jennifer had coveted when she and Michael had first started going out, back in the sixties.

Why had his wife hidden a captive bird in their garden shed, let alone a magpie? The garden was Jennifer's domain and he rarely encroached. Respect for his wife's privacy, he told himself, although he knew it was really a lack of interest. Michael understood the cause of his indifference: Jennifer's drinking, her ridiculous superstitious obsessions. This most recent discovery was just further evidence of her compulsive attention-seeking.

How long had she been hiding the bird? Hours? Days? No longer than that, surely? How did she manage to get it in here without him noticing? His wife was normally so house proud. He was amazed she would have something so 'dirty' anywhere near her.

The house was everything to Jennifer. He remembered her excitement when they first viewed the property all those years ago. Handsome and imposing, the grey Scottish sandstone lent an authority and austerity that appealed to them and reflected their ambitions. They found the East Neuk village charming, a delightful assortment of whitewashed cottages stacked together like fish boxes around a tiny harbour, with grand Victorian villas forming a protective outer ring. The location, over the Forth Bridge and a good thirty miles up the coast, required a lengthy commute by car and train into Edinburgh each day, but Michael knew that the house was far more lavish than anything he could afford in the capital. Perhaps they should have stayed in the city. But now it was too late, no one could ever persuade Jennifer to leave.

The magpie gave a long call of protest, a series of extended clicks rasping like an angry football rattle. The cage was much larger than the kind used for songbirds or even parrots. It was about three or four feet high and had several separate compartments, each with its own little entrance like some kind of bizarre avian hotel. The magpie was confined to an enclosure on the floor, an area larger than the others. Why on earth would his wife want to keep such a thing and why did she need such a large cage? Did she intend to collect birds of different species. But he was the collector, not his wife. Antique furniture, paintings, books, his precious clocks. It wasn't Jennifer's style at all.

With a push of his foot Michael slid the cage back, making sure it was positioned roughly as he had found it. Stepping out of the shed, he took a deep breath of fresh air, relieved to be out of the musty hut. He closed and padlocked the shed door. Reaching up to brush an insect from his face, he felt a slippery film of perspiration. He did not pause but turned and headed back up to the house. He needed to hurry if he were to replace the key on the rack in the cloakroom before his wife returned.

'OH GOOD DARLING, YOU'RE GETTING READY. You can help me get organised once you're done.'

Jennifer was standing in the middle of the spacious bathroom, her tone brisk and businesslike with no hint of duplicity or guilt. Having showered, Michael was drying himself, his skin hot and pink, rubbery to the touch. Wiping the steam from the mirror, he ran a hand through his hair, examining the ever-encroaching grey. Jennifer held a vase of hydrangeas freshly picked from the garden. She leant over the bath to fill the pot with water. Like him, she was putting on weight, although in her case all to the rear.

'Oh darling, don't say you've forgotten.'

'Forgotten what?' He knew perfectly well but it felt necessary to pretend.

'You have! James and Caroline. You know, for dinner. Tonight? *For goodness sake*. I reminded you at least twice last week.'

'Shit, of course.' He feigned sudden realisation. 'Don't worry, I'll be ready in a few minutes and then I'll give you a hand.'

When he came down Jennifer was frying some kidneys, a half-empty bottle of red beside her. They sizzled as she slopped in more wine before refilling her own glass without, Michael noted, offering any to him.

'Now, you're not going to cross-examine poor James again, are you? Honestly, you lawyers. Can never have a civilised dinner table conversation.' She smiled benignly as if scolding a child. 'It's always got to be point scoring. What is it with you two? And please stay off asylum seekers.' She looked at him pleadingly. '*Please?*'

'HERE YOU GO, MATE, SOME JUNGLE JUICE. For later on. It'll blow your socks off,' James winked as he thrust a labelless bottle into Michael's hand almost as soon as he opened the door. It was around eight, still warm and light outside. The younger man had just returned from another month in Africa, sorting out some trouble with the natives he said. He was deeply tanned, emphasised by his white open-necked shirt. Michael wondered just how hard he had been working while he was away. He greeted Caroline with a formal handshake. At the moment their fingers gripped, she tilted her head to one side, eyes smiling, and flicked her long hair across a smooth bare shoulder.

'Lovely to see you *again*, Michael.'

There was a good ten-year gap between the two couples. In fact James and Caroline seemed closer in age to Michael and Jennifer's daughter, Hannah. But like them, James and Caroline were in-comers to the village and didn't really mix with the locals. The two women met at a craft fair in the community hall. Jennifer had made an acerbic remark about one stallholder's 'floral fancies' and Caroline had tried in vain to stifle her giggles. They became firm friends almost immediately to Michael's considerable relief. Caroline was young and vivacious and Jennifer had been in desperate need of an ally ever since Hannah had left home to study.

'Lovely to see you both.' Jennifer greeted her guests with a kiss on the cheek. 'You'll excuse me won't you? We're almost ready. Michael, will you organise the drinks?'

He led them into the drawing room.

'So, how's the oil business, James?' Michael asked, handing his guests a gin and tonic each.

'Oh you know, the usual, boring stuff. Contracts and drilling rights. Just shuffling papers as always. Nothing like the bar, eh Michael? Theatre of the courtroom they call it, don't they? *Gowns, pounds and clowns* we used to say. No offence, mate?' James made no attempt to hide the smirk on his face.

Michael didn't rise to it. He didn't need to.

The meal was excellent. When it came to entertaining, Michael and Jennifer made a point of excelling. It started with a delicious French onion soup, Michael's speciality, a recipe he had picked up from an old chef while on holiday in the Carmargue a couple of years before. This was followed by the kidneys Jennifer had prepared earlier. As they ate they chatted about the village, compared stories. Jennifer reminded them how rude people could be in the shops, her favourite theme.

'It'd be bad enough if we were from somewhere else in Scotland other than Fife. But the fact that we're English.'

'Yes, it might even be okay if we were tourists,' said James.

'And they could rip us off,' Caroline added.

'But heaven forbid we actually *live* here,' Jennifer continued, 'they take it as a personal insult.'

Caroline talked about her time in London, her worries when she and James decided to move north. Jennifer sympathised and complained about how dismissive her old university friends had been when they had decided to return to Edinburgh, her husband's home town. They saw it as a lack of ambition, were even more sceptical when she and Michael moved across the Firth to the obscurity of the village, although they did their best to mask it behind smiles and enthusiasm.

'They're still the same,' Jennifer said collecting the plates. 'Always saying how lucky we are to be in such a quaint location, what a perfect life we have. How Michael's commute each day is nothing compared to what most people put up with down there, how dreadfully over-populated and congested the home counties are. How ridiculous the house prices have become.' She paused to take a swig from her glass. 'They go on about how Michael would need to be on at least five hundred thousand a year to afford what we have now. It's incredibly patronising.'

'God, that's so true,' Caroline said. 'We get the same. It's just their way of emphasising how much they earn and how isolated we are from what in their minds is the centre of the bloody universe.'

The main course was gamey: wood pigeon, pheasant or grouse in a sweet bramble sauce. Jennifer refused to confirm which it was. She became very mysterious and when they pressed she just beamed and told them to try and guess. Michael looked at her closely, thought she looked puffy, presumed she was half-pissed.

By coffee the conversation had turned to Michael's collections. James had left the table and was admiring a couple of pictures and a carriage clock that sat on the mahogany dresser.

'I like your taste, Michael.' He bent over and peered at one of the framed prints. 'Is this Chinese? It looks pretty old.'

'It's Japanese, late eighteenth century. A client introduced me to them a few years ago. Got bitten by the bug before they became really popular and the prices rose.'

James made a high-pitched whistling sound. 'Bet they're a good investment. Now *this* is a lovely piece.' He was running his hand along the smooth curves of the dresser. Victorian or Georgian?'

'Late eighteenth, I did some of the restoration myself. I've got a workshop in the attic. Just the occasional piece. It helps me relax.'

'Gosh. How clever of you.' Absent-mindedly, Caroline dipped a finger in her wine, and then, leaning on her elbows, slowly and deliberately sucked the digit clean. 'I didn't know you restored furniture, Michael.' She was a good liar. 'I'd love to see something. Can I get a look? I'm absolutely useless when it comes to practical things. You know, got thrown out of sewing class. Absolutely useless. But it's always so impressive when someone's good with their hands. Has a talent. Will you let me see, Michael? I'd love to have a look.'

Michael wondered if it was a good idea, thought it might be risky. 'There's not that much to look at just now. More a work-in-progress. Shall we go through and open that bottle you brought, James?'

'Oh, go on Michael, let her have a look,' Jennifer said. 'Let her see what you get up to…'

'Go on, mate. She loves that kind of stuff,' James chipped in. 'She's always dragging me into potteries and craft shops.'

MICHAEL MADE HIS WAY UP THE STAIRCASE with Caroline following closely behind, their steps soft on the thick cream carpet. On the landing, he opened a cupboard and pulled out a short wooden pole with a curling brass hook on the end and then reached up to a trap door in the ceiling. He gave a tug and pulled down the hatch. In turn this lowered a telescopic aluminium ladder. It gave a grating, metallic rasp as he pulled it down to the floor.

'After you, madam,' he said standing aside.

'Why thank you, kind sir.' Caroline smiled demurely and gave a mock curtsey before climbing up the steps into the attic.

Although the remnants of daylight were visible through the skylight, it was still dark in the roof space. He found the light switch. Several pieces of furniture in various stages of restoration were revealed, boxes of books piled to the rafters and other assorted junk. The air was muggy, the roof slates having retained the heat of the day. In one corner there was a chaise lounge, its burgundy plush worn through in several places, allowing coarse horsehair to spill out untidily. In another a snap table had been recently stripped and was ready for polishing. A wardrobe in five or six pieces lay across the floor.

Caroline walked around, hands on hips proprietarily, her heels tapping lightly on the bare floorboards. She walked under the skylight, for a moment the receding sunlight bathing her hair and shoulders in a golden aura. She flicked through some paintings that were stacked against a joist.

'What are these? They look interesting.' She lifted out a small oil painting in a heavy gilt frame. A woman lay naked on a rock, surrounded by seaweed, the waves crashing over her prone limbs.

'Oh, just some old stuff I got years ago from galleries in Edinburgh. Not exactly quality, mostly turn of the century, Celtic Renaissance, harking back to the old mythologies. It's more like Jennifer's thing. That's what's known as a Kelpie.'

'A what?'

'A Scottish superstition, bit like a mermaid. It was all I could afford in my younger days,' he said in mitigation.

Caroline replaced the picture and returned to the centre of the room looking intently at Michael as she did so.

'Well, I can see you're quite the collector.' She slipped her arms around his waist and pulled him towards her, close enough for him to smell her scent. 'Quite the dirty old magpie.' She pulled back for a moment and looked around the attic once more. 'I expect this is where I'll end up one day, when you've grown tired of me. You'll store me away with the other things you've lost interest in. Replaced by something new and shiny that catches your eye.'

When they came back downstairs, Michael and Caroline found the dining room empty. They looked in the kitchen half expecting the others had made a start on the dishes. But the plates and cutlery were piled on top of each other on the polished granite worktop waiting patiently to be rinsed and stacked in the dishwasher. They checked the drawing room and found nothing but James's liqueur bottle. Michael lifted it from the coffee table, leaving a brown sticky ring on the otherwise spotless surface. It had been opened and, judging by the weight in his hand, was now only half full.

The French windows were open and it was clear from the muffled voices outside that Jennifer had taken her guest out into the garden to show off her pride and joy. They made their way out onto the patio and found their respective spouses sitting under the laburnum drinking in the half-light.

'There you both are.' Caroline greeted them. 'We couldn't find you anywhere.'

'I see you've got stuck into James's bottle of rocket fuel or whatever he called it,' said Michael.

'Jungle juice, mate,' James reminded him. 'Best in bloody Africa.'

'And you two took so long we had no option but to get stuck in.' Jennifer flashed Michael a look he did not recognise, alien and aggressive. She turned to James, nudged him with an elbow, and they laughed conspiratorially like school children.

'Well, you better slow down and let us catch you up,' said Caroline, returning from inside having collected the bottle and two more glasses.

'*Au contraire*, mademoiselle, I think it is we who must catch up with you,' Jennifer replied in a cold foreign accent, winking at her companion, before dissolving into giggles again.

Michael watched his wife with the care of a zookeeper in a cage with an unpredictable wild animal. She was spoiling for a fight and was relishing the audience.

'Anyway,' she announced. 'James was telling me all about the birds in Africa. 'He's a bit of an…'

'Ornithologist,' James helped out. 'Strictly part-time. Not one of the beardy-weirdy brigade.'

'Yes, he's a bird fancier. You know, fancies the birds…'

'I was just telling your lovely wife how beautiful the birds are in West Africa.'

'And I was telling him about all the lovely birds we get in our garden. We do, darling, don't we?' Jennifer gestured with her glass towards Michael, the brown liquid slopping around inside, splashing over the rim. 'Lots of lovely birds. Finches, wrens and tits.' She sniggered as she said the word before recovering herself. 'A jay or two sometimes. We even had owls nesting for a couple of years, under the eves of the garage. Hannah got so excited when she saw the little baby chicks.'

For a moment Michael thought Jennifer would turn maudlin and tearful over her daughter, lost to adulthood and independence. 'That was a very long time ago, Jennifer.'

But she only paused to take breath. 'And sea birds, lots of sea birds here of course. Waders and oyster catchers. But I do love the swallows and house martins best of all. Don't I Michael? They're so beautiful the way they fly.' She made the movement with her arm theatrically. 'Swooping up and down. Like this. Up and down, over the garden, up and down.'

'Yes. I think we've got the idea.' Michael said, looking across to Caroline, hoping for some assistance.

'What do you know?' Jennifer replied. 'You don't pay a blind bit of notice to what goes on in this garden, do you my dear?' She grinned sarcastically. 'Too busy grubbing about up in that attic of yours, playing with your precious flotsam and jetsam, other people's cast-offs. You wouldn't know a swallow if it flew up and pecked you on the arse.'

'What about magpies? You must get lots of lovely magpies in this garden.' Caroline tried to change the subject. 'I love magpies. They're like the harlequins of the bird world, don't you think? So cheeky, always up to mischief.'

Jennifer's countenance changed, clouded over with comical distaste like the face of child about to spit out unpleasant medicine. '*Oh, god no!* We don't like magpies here. Ghastly birds. God no, we don't like them at all. Terrible things, magpies. Thieves and murderers, every one.'

'Sound like your clients, eh Michael?' said James, having drained his glass.

'I thought the stealing was just an old wives tale.' Caroline pulled her cardigan over her shoulders.

'They take things alright. Clothes pegs, plant tags, anything they can get their dirty little beaks on. But what's worse, they kill young songbirds, murder them in their nests when they're still chicks. Throw them out of the nest and take it over. They're too lazy and degenerate to build their own. I've seen them do it. Three young blackbirds, too young even for proper feathers. So small and vulnerable. Thrown out of a nest and lying discarded on the ground at the foot of a tree, like old rubbish. I found them myself.'

'I think perhaps you're talking rubbish,' Michael said with a forced laugh.

'I am not.' Jennifer replied acidly. 'Ask the orni-fucking-thologist,'

James smirked. 'Well, yes. I think there may be some truth in that but I can't imagine it has any lasting effect. Even if it seems that magpies are on the increase these days.'

'See?' Jennifer turned to Michael in triumph. 'And I haven't even started on how unlucky they are. They're cursed birds, harbingers of wrong-doing.'

'Oh Christ, not this again. Now you're just being ridiculous.' Michael didn't like the direction the conversation was going, had an idea where Jennifer might be headed.

'No, they are sent here to spread pain and unhappiness. Centuries of people have seen those bloody birds and hated them for it.'

Michael couldn't stand it any longer, couldn't stand the humiliation. The amused look on James's face, his smug little glances over to his wife. He tried to suppress his anger, tried not to descend to Jennifer's level, but he could not help himself.

'Then why the hell have you got one stored in the bloody garden shed?' he yelled. 'If you hate the things so much why the hell have you got one in a cage down there, in your stupid bloody garden shed?'

Jennifer became quiet, leaned forward with her elbows on her knees. 'Ah-ha,' she said, tapping her nose. 'You found her then.'

'Yes, I sodding-well found it…' He turned to Caroline. 'Can you believe that my wife has been keeping a magpie? Don't you think this somewhat undermines your case, Jennifer? Where the hell did you get it?'

'From a farmer. He was very helpful. Found him on the Internet. What an amazing thing the Internet is. You can find almost anything you want on the World Wide Web.' She winked at James.

'But you still haven't told us what the hell you need the stupid bird for. Is it some kind of ridiculous pet?'

'No, you idiot. It's for sorting them out. All the others…'

'What others, Jennifer?' Caroline asked in sympathetic tones, the kind normally reserved for an unreasonable toddler.

'I use it in the trap. My trap. You need a female to attract others. You can't catch them otherwise. I'm finally doing something useful. Ridding the world of those bastard birds. I know what you are up to, Michael.' Jennifer paused and looked directly at Caroline, fixing her with a vicious glare. 'Why else would there be so many. Hundreds of them, coming to destroy what we've created, coming to ruin everything we have striven to build, the life we've made together. Here, in this house. In *my* garden.'

'Hang on a minute, mate,' James said. 'Am I missing something here?'

'Shut up you idiot.' Jennifer interrupted. 'All of you, follow me.' She got up and left the patio, disappearing round the side of the house. Meekly, Michael and his guests followed. The night was warm, the midsummer sky not black but an inky blue, only the brightest stars visible.

They found Jennifer at the back door. 'Wait here,' she demanded before disappearing into the house. 'I'll only be a minute,' came a disembodied voice from inside. The light above the garage came on, illuminating a swarm of insects that danced erratically in the halo of its glow. Jennifer reappeared with a silver key, which she inserted into a lock in the handle of the garage door. With a wrench, she hauled it up and over her head.

It was the smell that hit them first. They could not see anything immediately. The brilliance of the exterior light projected outward, the angle of the sliding door shading the interior, trapping in the darkness. But the smell, the stench of rancid meat, the reek of rotting matter mixed with bird shit, rose in their nostrils and stung the back of their throats like acid.

Jennifer moved inside the garage and in a moment turned on the single bare bulb that hung from the ceiling. In the stark cold light, birds, magpies Michael realised, dead magpies, were hanging from every rafter. Dozens, maybe as many as a hundred, perhaps more. They hung, bedraggled, like a vast collection of broken umbrellas, spokes askew, savagely ripped and torn by the wind and rain. Clumps of black and white feathers littered the floor. The birds had been suspended by the legs with green garden wire, their twisted feet pointed upwards in a bizarre and simultaneous salute.

'What the hell...?' Michael said in an almost inaudible whisper, as he walked inside the garage, gazing upwards at the grotesque funereal decoration.

'Oh my God,' was all Caroline could manage as she followed, before clasping both hands to her mouth, her cheeks bulging. James, by her side, was incredulous.

'What the hell is going on, Michael? Is this some kind of sick joke?

'No joke.' Jennifer replied. 'As you can see, I've done pretty well. I make no apology for what I've been doing, even if it's only a drop in the ocean, a small victory in the war against this... this... *pestilence*. There have been a lot more than you see here. I've been at it a while.' She smiled sweetly. 'It just goes to show how much attention you pay, darling, doesn't it?'

Michael didn't reply.

'I've disposed of the others in different ways,' she continued. 'The council have been most helpful. And you three have done your bit. You all enjoyed tonight's meal didn't you?'

At that moment Caroline threw up, emptied the contents of her stomach in great heaving convulsions onto the smooth concrete floor. Jennifer looked pleased, arms folded, proud of her handiwork.

'What are you two playing at?' James demanded, his hand resting on his wife's back as she bent, her eyes and nose streaming. 'Whatever you're up to, whatever sick game you're playing, we don't want to be part of it.' He turned and began to lead the now sobbing Caroline out into the fresh air, away from the putrid spectacle. He paused at the threshold, looked round at Michael and Jennifer. But he shook his head, bewildered. 'What the hell is this all about? Fuck! What is wrong with you people, *for god's sake*? I mean to say... just look at yourselves!'

WAITING TILL THE LIGHT FROM THE BEDROOM WINDOW had dimmed, Michael returned to the shed. The magpie fluttered a little as he carried the cage through the garden but otherwise remained mute, silenced by the darkness. At the patio, he settled the bird on an upturned planter, checking to make sure the cage was stable. Although it remained quiet, the magpie was alert to the nocturnal sounds all around. As he sat down he could feel the chill of the flagstones through the thin fabric of his trousers despite the warmth of the night air.

A breeze toyed at Michael's ankles, gentle fingers brushing lightly across the bare skin of his arms, the hairs rising slightly at the sensation. Hoping to keep moths and other insects at bay, he took out a cigarette, no more than an occasional indulgence these days. He struck a match. It flared and fizzed like a tiny firework before he flicked it in a looping arc across the patio. Its glow remained visible in the shrubbery for only a moment before it faded and died. He inhaled deeply, enjoying the burn of nicotine in his nostrils. Something stirred in him, an echo and remembrance of a youth long departed.

As he sat there, threads of grey-blue smoke twisting upwards into the gloom, he tried to remember, tried to visualise Jennifer as he had first known her, all those years ago. A skinny girl of twenty-one, soon to graduate, wide-eyed, full of life and intelligence, brimming with laughter and optimism.

He tried to recall those earliest days, when they started seeing each other, first date as his daughter's generation now called it. He remembered punting on the river, thought back, trying to conjure an image. Two bodies lying together in the base of a boat, languid in each other's arms, flowing with the current, a hand trailing in the water as willows reached down like curtains from either bank. What had they done then? He guessed a meal in a cheap restaurant, candle-lit and intimate, but not much else, all he could afford on his meagre student grant. Then walking home arm in arm, only to linger on the doorstep perhaps, lacking a common vocabulary, not yet knowing how to say goodnight.

In truth, it was all hazy, smudged and blurred by time. His memory had gone dark. He could hardly recognise himself or who he had been, let alone the girl who had become his wife, the woman with whom he had built this life and shared so many years.

Michael wondered how he had felt when they had first made love. Had he been clumsy, inept? He did not think so. More likely he had admired her like a precious jewel, examined her with intensity reserved only for the rarest artefact, cherished her jealously.

He opened the door of the cage and reached inside, slowly cupping both hands around the bird. He carefully drew the magpie out and then held it on his lap, marvelling at the texture of the feathers, the warmth of its body against his palms.

Yes. A memory, a recollection. Emerging in fragments, like an old painting hidden under layers of opaque and yellowed lacquer, slowly cleaned to reveal the forgotten colours beneath.

They had lain together silently, somewhere, he could not remember where. Darkness, the quiet beat of music from a radio turned down low, the coarse texture of the blanket beneath them, the rhythm of traffic on wet streets outside. A single bed, huddled together, gripping each other tightly. Shy and fearful of one another and yet, at the same time, alive with sensation, burning with the electricity of hope and expectation.

DEAN FRANCIS ALFAR

Hollow Girl: A Romance

I

HOLLOW GIRL FIRST BECAME AWARE OF SOUND: a sudden thumping that repeated itself in an established rhythm. Without anything else to focus on, she was entranced, mesmerized by the regular beating of her heart. When vision came, her world exploded in light: colors and shapes that fought for her attention, swirling into clarity before being disrupted by the next image. Touch followed: the waft of warm recycled air from the atmospheric scrubbers on her skinsheath, the cool moisture on her face, the gentle caress of the polyfabrics that swathed her body in lieu of a mother's embrace.

"Can you hear me?" A voice rasped from somewhere to her left, the question pushing the nanotech in her brain to lightning activity.

"Yes," Hollow Girl said, marveling momentarily at the resonance of her voice, the vibration in her throat, and the motion of her tongue and lips.

"Can you sit up?" The voice asked, as she felt her birthing cocoon removed, band by band.

"Yes," she said, sitting up slowly, without pausing to consider the meaning of the request. She felt the flex of her muscles culminating with a tightness centered on her stomach.

"*Kamusta*," said the man who stood next to her, his face emanating an almost desperate manner of kindness. "If you feel nauseous, you may lie back. Do you feel dizzy?"

"No," Hollow Girl replied, surprised at the way her head shook from side to side. She did not feel any degree of discomfort at all, with the exception of a growing sense of embarrassment provoked by her nudity.

"May I have some clothing?" she asked, facing the man who was concerned with her well-being. His head was shaven and square-shaped, his eyes a dull brown.

"Of course, of course," he replied, vanishing for a moment behind a pale blue curtain before returning with folded clothing in his arms. "*Eto*," he said, handing the small pile over to her.

Hollow Girl accepted his offering and wordlessly swung her feet off the birthing crèche. Her soles registered only the most insubstantial cold before the Romblontech tiles provided a pre-calculated amount of heat. She wore the short dress and stood before the short man for approval.

"*Ayan, ayan*," the man exclaimed in delight. "You're just perfect."

✤   ✤   ✤

IN THE DAYS THAT FOLLOWED, Hollow Girl grew at an astonishing rate, surprising even the man whom she came to know as her creator.

"It's all there inside your head," he told her once, as she watched him pick at his lunch: okra, water chestnuts, and squash with a dash of sour cream. "Ninety-eight percent of each of your brain cells has been engineered to hold enormous amounts of preselected information. Every book that has ever been catalogued is there inside."

She looked at him and carefully asked, "Then why do I feel empty?"

"Empty?" he repeated, stabbing at an obstinate water chestnut. "What an absurd question. You are anything but empty. You are filled to the brim with magnitudes of information. You have the best the Philippines—no, the best the world has to offer."

She watched him without expression, quietly determining the precise trajectory required for her creator's fork to spear his target as she tried to assess the vacancy within her that she had attempted to articulate.

"May I have a name?" she asked him as he finished his meal.

"If you feel so strongly about it, then choose one for yourself," he replied, scratching at the rash behind his ears.

She thought for a moment then said, "Hollow Girl."

⊕ ⊕ ⊕

IN THE MONTHS THAT PASSED, Hollow Girl assisted her creator in his work, giving him complete access to her abundant stored information. They quickly established a certain working order, with her standing next to him as he struggled, in bursts of patriotic zeal, to conquer the scientific mysteries that eluded him.

"We do what we do for our country," he said grandly. "There was a time when the Philippines was considered the beggar of Asia, but thankfully, that time is in the distant past. But there are still things to be discovered, secrets to pry from the silence of nature."

"Why do you look for so many answers?" she asked him.

"Why do you ask so many questions?" he asked her back.

In that moment, Hollow Girl realized that she shared more in common with her creator than simple existence, and her feeling of emptiness grew and an inconceivable vacuum established itself in her heart.

"Today, I plan to make myself small enough to explore a blood vessel," he told her, pointing to the apparatus he had assembled with her help. "Think of the things I'll see."

"I will have to leave you soon," she told him, her words heavy with sorrow.

He didn't answer her, busying himself with the components of his miniaturized experiment: ship, suit, helmet, recorders, clock, and cigarette— all emblazoned with tiny Philippine flags.

"Do you mean now?" he asked her, when he realized she was still waiting for him to speak. "We still have much to do."

"I have questions neither of us can answer," she told him.

"*O, sige,*" he nodded. "But do you have time for one last thing?"

⊕   ⊕   ⊕

HE RODE THE KNIFE AS IT SLASHED TOWARDS HOLLOW GIRL, the rush of air muffled by the null-audits of his helmet. Still, he felt the sound, the sibilance crashing over his miniaturized compartment at the blade's sharpest point as he cut through the space between them. Around him, nanotech cameras recorded the approach, the digital images they captured streaming across the impossible gulf and saved for posterity in the huge J/Banico servers in his laboratory.

As he neared the break point, he could not help but blanch at the inelegant terrain that was Hollow Girl's skinsheath. At his size, flesh tones defined the sky and the horizon, and follicles towered like sullen gods forced to kenosis. He allowed himself a smile at the detail of his creation.

He adjusted the cameras for optimal perspective, wanting every possible shot, every possible angle of entry—to remember her by, he thought, in a moment of peculiar sadness.

He checked his harnesses and helmet one last time as he prepared for impact, confronted by a yawning emptiness before the knife tip made contact with Hollow Girl. For a moment, it was as if nothing else would happen—in that exquisite moment before the inevitable, he realized the symbolism of his act of penetration.

Her skinsheath gave way, diaphanous and irrelevant—a tear, exposing the wonders beneath her epidermis before the blood reacted, welling up, flooding out in a single eternal globule, black and blacker from his viewpoint.

And his ride continued, cutting deeper within Hollow Girl. Darkness was replaced by the lambent glow of his cockpit lights, and as he found himself embraced by the hot wound, the temperature in his capsule adjusted to accommodate the heat outside the blade.

He commanded the cameras to 3D-mode, orientating ellipses, making panoramic cycles of motion, enslaving everything that could be seen.

II

HOLLOW GIRL LOOKED AT HER REFLECTION IN THE MIRROR of the restroom of the New Davao Club for Men. Her eyes had changed color again, overnight: russet and grey replacing yesterday's lilac. She ran some warm water and wet her hands, then her face, watching the droplets trail down her features, tracing the contour of her cheekbones towards the angle of her jaw line and down the tip of her chin.

"*Alam mo*, sometimes I think you're too beautiful for your own good," k8lin said, moving beside Hollow Girl. k8lin was a head taller, with close-cropped black hair that accentuated her Filichino looks.

"I wasn't admiring myself," Hollow Girl said in an even tone. She had gotten used to all the intrigue and sniping of every other masseuse at the Club, and though k8lin's words were barbed, Hollow Girl knew that they were empty as well.

"*Ewan ko ba* why we even bother," k8lin said, stripping off an eyebrow with one stroke. "When it's time for sex, most of them close their eyes anyway." She opened her vanity kit, selected a replacement eyebrow, and applied it, twitching the muscles of her forehead to make sure it held.

"I like it when they look into my eyes," Hollow Girl said softly.

"Right," k8lin said, turning away from the mirror to look at Hollow Girl directly. "And I'm here because I love what I do."

The mirror shimmered and the pixelized image of Triple M, Matron M-lani Marquez, appeared, her voice rendered in dulcet audio.

"Holly," the image said, "Your fingers are needed."

⊕ ⊕ ⊕

HOLLOW GIRL'S CLIENT WAS POSITIONED ON HIS STOMACH, his head pressed against the thin red pillow. Her fingers pressed against his back, her touch firm yet oddly light, engaging his skin and muscles in a pattern of give-and-take

The man lost all sense of time, trapped between the eternal moment of pressure and release, a repeating pattern of rhythmic motion, as his skin surrendered all intimate knowledge of its secret aches and places to her fingers and palms.

"Sir, may I ask you a question," she said, as he was enveloped in the scent of oil, thick and cold at first but dramatically rendered airy and warm by the conversion of her touch.

The man tried to answer but could not form a single coherent thought, reduced instead to a self-conscious moan.

"What can you tell me about love?" she asked, moving her fingers down his spine, counting each vertebra as she coaxed them into feeling. She paused then to pour more oil onto the small of his back and the curvature of his buttocks, denying the liquid any routes of escape by quickly rubbing it into his skin.

Helplessly, the man felt his unbidden arousal as she sought deep muscle in tight focused circles. He tried to shift position to relieve his discomfort, but her fingers rode his motion like old seafarers sailing in familiar oceans, adjusting, adapting, never breaking their union of skin.

"Do you expect to find it here?" Hollow Girl said, changing the texture of her skinsheath as she leaned over and massaged his shoulders.

"Come home with me," the man finally managed to say. "I will show you."

⊕   ⊕   ⊕

THREE YEARS LATER, HE CAME HOME TO FIND Hollow Girl at the door of their apartment in Mega Makati, waiting to say goodbye.

"What's going on? Where are you going?" he asked, despite already knowing the answer.

"I wanted to give you my key," she said, handing him the sensekey. "There's some food in the Omnitop—you just need to decide if you want to have bread or make some rice."

"Please don't go."

Hollow Girl looked at him with her gold-flecked eyes, and in that instant, everything he loved about her was reflected in the measure of her gaze.

"Don't. Don't cry. Please." She kissed him on the cheek and held his face in her hands.

"But why? Tell me why," he asked her. His entire body felt like it wasn't his own. It was too heavy, too solid, too real to be real in that unreality where the world existed but was of no substance.

"Goodbye."

"Why?"

"Because I have too many questions."

He watched her walk away, down the brightly lit hall to the airshaft. He wanted to run after her, to beg, to plead, to try everything, say anything, but the unwelcome gravity of the situation was too strong to fight, to struggle against. Instead, he watched her turn towards him one last time as the airshaft signaled its availability, watched her vanish behind its invisible caress, watched the ghost of her last smile disperse like the illusion that it was, and stared down numbly at the sensekey in his hand.

He was oddly flooded with thoughts of particles in motion in a void; of black holes suspended in infinite black space and of the loneliness of their existence—invisible, powerful, devouring, in solitude; of stars that suddenly flare and supernova, brilliant, burning, echoing light for millions of years, and of worlds that spin unaware that the source of their light is long dead, long gone, a corpse-light. He wanted to cry, to shout, to articulate his pain but realized it was pointless, because words, like sound, could not exist in the vacuum of her departure.

III

HOLLOW GIRL FOUND WORK, DOING RAPID ANALYSIS and calculations, on the AsiaPac community station in geosynch orbit around the sunside of the moon. The hours were long but her circumstances, like the spin-generated gravity, suited her well.

During the artificial night cycles, she found solace in Tranquil, a subtle narcotic blend that she injected directly into the tiny aperture behind her left ear, allowing her to manipulate the stuff of her dreams. She knew it was destroying her but she felt that she needed the calm it bestowed.

Gabriel-Four, an enhanced man, had begun courting her from the moment she first set foot on the station, four years ago.

"It's not so bad being what we are," he told her, curling and uncurling his multiple limbs. He was engineered for physical multi-tasking but was made redundant when the need for such specialists vanished in the wake of another ergonomic discovery. "The trick, I guess, is finding something else to do."

"The trick is in finding the reason for the trick," Hollow Girl said.

"But that would be like understanding how an illusion works," Gabriel-Four replied. "Don't you think that sometimes it's better just to sit back and marvel at the show?"

"I can't just watch," she said. "Too many people do just that."

"Then what would you do?" he asked her.

"I want to fall in love," she said simply.

"Then fall in love with me," he replied.

"I have left every man who has ever loved me," Hollow Girl whispered quietly into his ear.

"I will take what I can," he said with a brittle smile.

"Do you believe that someone who has no heart can truly love?"

In the ensuing void of words, Gabriel-Four kissed Hollow Girl gently on her dry lips and pretended they were as moist as the tears that fell from his eyes.

She broke from the kiss and turned her face away to cough, hiding in the cup of her palm the flecks of virtual blood that came with distressing frequency. But he saw it, as he had seen through all the previous times of her subterfuge, and again chose not to call attention to it.

"I'm tired," she said.

"I love you, Hollow Girl," Gabriel-Four said as she walked away. Whatever elation he should have felt at that moment seemed as hollow as the object of his adoration. As he watched her leave, he realized how sometimes devotion was a curse, imperceptible and relentless in the consumption of hope.

SHE DECIDED THAT NIGHT TO DREAM OF HER CREATOR.

They were standing next to each other, her birthing crèche adjacent to their flickering bodies. She imagined him young and so he was young, smiling and benevolent. She imagined herself as herself during that time, and it was not very difficult because so little about her had truly changed.

"Why did you make me this way?" she asked him.

"Why are you so obsessed with love?" he asked her. "It's unhealthy."

"Why can't I be happy?" she questioned.

"Why do you think love is the answer?" he said.

"Because love is what I do not have," she replied. "It is the only thing I do not understand."

"*Talaga*," her creator raised an eyebrow. "Of all the myriad mysteries of the universe, love is the only thing you do not understand? I must have built you better than I thought."

"You did not build me with what it takes to understand," she said.

"Listen," he said. "I built you just fine. Now wake up and start living your life. You have too many questions."

⊕ ⊕ ⊕

HOLLOW GIRL FOUND GABRIEL-FOUR ASLEEP IN HIS CUBICLE, his arms dangling from his pallet. His face was handsome in the dim light, his features enhanced by the play of shadows.

He opened his eyes and saw her standing at the doorway. Wordlessly, he shifted his body to make room for her on the narrow bed, and then gestured for her to come.

She closed her eyes for a moment before joining him, and when she felt his arms around her it felt like she was coming across an unfamiliar word for the first time. She recognized the letters, could guess at the sense of it, but knew absolutely nothing of its meaning. Her intelligence wrestled with the notion of staring at something whose significance she should have been aware of, context or no context, but she was reduced to conjecture, lost in the heat of semiotics.

Gabriel-Four watched her sit beside him, watching her eyes shift colors with every second.

"Are you—" he began to ask.

"Shhh," Hollow Girl said, with a smile on her face, listening to the beating of their hearts.

Iain Maloney

Things I Know Are True Because Hollywood Says So.

You'd better be ready. Seven o'clock remember. I'll ring twice.

I hang up. Hand still on the receiver I rest my head against the wall. The painkillers no longer deal with the headaches. It feels like my eyeball is being forced out. I swivel so my back is to the wall and sink to the floor. Everything important has been done: just the trivial things left. That's where things will go wrong. Something small is liable to slip the net.

How long has the CD been skipping? I listen to the disc slipping, trying to work out at which point. In films it always sticks at an ideal part of the song, the ironic repeated phrase but not in real life. CD's don't repeat phrases, only vinyl. CD's just make an annoying tick tick tick interminably like a metronome. It isn't helping the headache. I wonder how long it'll take for the irritation to rise to the level necessary for action. Not long. I get up and fall through the open door of the lounge.

My flat's nice. It's quite small but then this isn't New York where large, loft-style apartments are well within the price range of most people—whether they are employed or not. But this suits me. I used to love this room. It's such a mess now, the walls nicotine stained, papers spread over the floor. The curtains haven't been open for months.

I think deciding to work from home was a mistake. The people at work were so jealous. I did what everyone dreams of doing: work from home, no boss looking over your shoulder, no commuting, and no office politics. No structure. Slapping the open/close button I stare at the row of discs along the mantlepiece. Decisions. The CD LED flashes 00:00. It looks like a bomb. All bombs are fitted with electronic timing devices with large red readouts so you know exactly when they're going to go off.

I select The Beatles, the White Album. As usual the disc isn't in the box so, straining like an old man, I get onto my knees and start searching through the carpet of silver plastic that surrounds the stereo.

It was fun at first. I installed all the relevant technology, geared myself up. Got the best of everything: the kind of laptop powerful enough to override the communications system of any invading alien society, and run applications everyone is familiar with.

I was a film reviewer for the local paper. I got paid to watch films and then complain about them—I'm that type of reviewer: every silver lining has a cloud. Soon I realised that I could get any movie on the Internet before its release. I would never have to go to the cinema again, never have to suffer the chatting, fidgeting and munchings, the forced plasticity of the whole experience. I could lie on my sofa, alone in silence and work. I could stop the film for a toilet break. I could smoke. I could eat real food. It was perfect.

I find the disk and insert it, hitting shuffle. Disc one, *I'm So Tired*. Maybe this kind of thing does happen in real life. I've got to get ready. I'll probably not sleep tonight. Should've got another prescription but it's too late now. Hopefully they'll have pills at the clinic. Hopefully they'll give me pills at the clinic. They'd better considering the price. How can Iceland be so expensive? It's hardly an economic power. Maybe that's the reason. I wish I knew more about Iceland. At least they'll all speak English. When they are alone, all foreigners prefer to speak English to each other. Should've rented more films. The only one I could find was *101 Reykjavik*, which isn't going to help too much. Everything you need to know can be found in films.

To begin with I revelled in the fact that I had no need to set the alarm, could rise when I wanted, go to work naked. After a while I began to sleep on the sofa with the phone in one hand, the remote in the other. I ordered all my food, paying by credit card. I watched films all day, sometimes watching the same one seven or eight times straight. It's strange how the mind works. If you have no reason to leave the house, you won't. If you have the technology, there is no need. All my work, banking, daily nutritional requirements could be achieved via the phone and the Internet. The video shop would deliver and collect my films. During the day I kept the curtains closed so the sunlight wouldn't interfere with the screen.

My mother took my films away. She came round eventually. I missed Christmas, she never saw me on my birthday. It was always just the two of us——an only child and a divorcee. I'm glad I didn't have a twin: at least one in a pair of identical twins is born evil. I never saw anything wrong with the way I was living. I was happy. She said I smelt dead. I no longer washed or changed. She called in someone who killed my pet mouse. She took me to the doctor who gave me pills. She took away my films.

I love my mother. I lived with her until I was twenty-eight. She cried when I moved out. She came round every day with food for me. She got upset when I stopped answering the door. She panicked. People always said she was over-protective. I don't see how that can be the case; surely over-protective is just extra careful. It was always just the two of us. She just didn't want anything bad happening to her only child.

I got fired. I submitted a review for a film which had been released in America but which was not being distributed over here. They were unhappy that I hadn't been going to the cinema, said I hadn't been entering into the spirit of things. I told them that I had been watching the films, that it made no difference where I watched them. I told them it showed that we were at the cutting edge, reviewing films that our readers hadn't seen. They said I'd betrayed their faith in me.

My mother found out about the clinic from a friend. I have problems distinguishing between reality and fantasy. Apparently they specialise in treating my condition. A new breakthrough in scientific understanding, a revolutionary technique. It is expensive but she says she can afford it. It is called Overlook and is out in the middle of nowhere. The brochure looks nice. It doesn't look like a hospital, more a kind of health farm. Mum says they can help me. They were unclear as to how long it would take so we're letting out my flat. She's going to deal with it all so I don't have to worry. I've never flown before but I'm not scared: if anything goes wrong I know I can take over: it's easy to land a plane providing there is someone in the control tower to talk you down. I wish mum could come. She hasn't flown since her honeymoon. She says it's amazing. If you go high enough you can see where the sky stops being blue and becomes black. Space. I wanted to be an astronaut when I was young. It's beautiful up there with the spaceships dancing.

I would like to leave in the evening rather than the morning. The hero always rides off into the sunset. It is only in the horror genre that people emerge into the dawn, stare up at the new sun glad that the demons are gone. I don't want to be the hero in a horror film. I want to be in an intelligent comedy where I have a few mishaps along the way but can look back on them and laugh. I walk through to the kitchen as *Don't Pass Me By* begins. On the table is a plate of mince and tatties with cling film covering it. I am to heat it up in the microwave. Radiation causes interesting mutations, not to your future children, but to you, right then and there, or over a period of time until you finally go crazy and kill people.

The headache is still there. I rake through the top drawer to find some paracetemol though I know there isn't any. The headaches started when I began taking the pills, a side effect. Mum said I could cope with them if they made me better. I suppose she's right but it doesn't make them any easier to suffer. They make my hands shake. What do I still have to do? I have a list somewhere. My suitcases are packed; mum has my passport and tickets. I won't need much money while I'm there but she changed about a hundred quid for me just in case.

At first I found it hard to live without films. I didn't know how to fill my day. I scanned magazines like Empire and Total Film, marking the new releases I was missing. I wandered aimlessly around the flat, restless, unhappy. One day I tried to go to the cinema. Mum had asked me not to but I couldn't help it anymore, I needed to see something. My life, my head was empty without them. At this point I hadn't been outside for about six months. I had a shower, put on clothes that she had cleaned for me. I felt good. I couldn't get beyond the end of the path. I stood, I don't know how long, at the gate unable to open it. When my mum came around after work she found me there. I don't know why I couldn't get any further. The idea of the cinema scared me. The thought of all those people intruding on my viewing made me shake. The idea of the world, a world that didn't follow the rules of film was terrifying. There wouldn't be clues as to what would happen next, there would be no climax to build towards. It simply happened, completely unscripted. I didn't try again. After that I found it much easier to fill my time and I only left the house with my mother. We went to the park a lot. It's right behind my flat, through the gate in the back garden. It's big enough that I can watch what's going on without taking part. I stand at the gate and it's all spread in front of me like a giant Imax screen.

My mother blamed herself for my dependency on movies. My father left us while I was in the cinema watching Star Wars. He dropped me off saying he'd pick me up after. When the film ended he was nowhere to be seen but my mother was sitting in the foyer crying. I went to see Star Wars every day while it was out. He never met me. I never saw him again. If someone says, "I'll be right back," they won't.

I want to see Star Wars just now. It always calmed me down. I should really go to bed. I don't like my bed—it's not comfy and the sheets are wrong. All beds have special L-shaped sheets that reach up to the armpit level on a woman but only to waist level on the man lying beside her. Not mine.

Mum says that even if I don't sleep just lying in bed will rest my body. I don't think that's true. I am always too restless to rest. I haven't slept naturally since she took the films away. I think I sleep sometimes. Within seconds the clock will have moved forward by hours. When you turn out the light to go to bed, everything in your bedroom will still be clearly visible, just slightly bluish. I must sleep sometimes; the doctor says I'd be dead otherwise. But he gave me pills to help. I slept a lot until they ran out. I kept forgetting to go back. I like being awake at night anyway. It's much more peaceful than daytime. As long as I'm ready for seven it'll be fine. It's good to have that kind of structure.

After making coffee I go out into the garden and stand at the gate. The sun is setting but it is not yet dark. The park is circular, bordered by trees and houses. During the day it is busy with children and dogs, at night it is home to tramps. It is not a safe place to be. I sip my coffee and watch. I am not of the scene; I am the audience, the camera. I am the director. As the light fades a man in a suit enters from the left. He is dishevelled. He is carrying a large rucksack and a heavy suitcase. He is crossing the grass with some purpose, heading deliberately for the large clump of trees opposite me. The only other person in the park is a tramp asleep on a bench. This is very suspicious. I run back into the flat and get my camera. It has a large, powerful zoom lens. Back at the gate I train the camera on the trees. The man has dropped the bags and is digging, half-hidden by the Copper Beech. I don't know what to do. Should I go over? Should I phone the police? Should I phone Mum?

I start snapping, the camera freezing the moment before he continues digging. He stops, throws down the shovel and wipes his brow. Snap. He drags the suitcase to the hole. Snap. He pushes it in. Snap. The rucksack follows. Snap. This is it. Something is finally happening. All the years my life was normal. All those disappointments. My headache has gone. The light is blue. He begins to fill in the hole and I begin to run, slow motion, across the grass. I can hear music. From a window somewhere *A Day In The Life* is playing:

I saw a film today, oh boy.

As I near him he sees me, steps away from the hole, raises the shovel above his head.

Luis Joaquin M. Katigbak

Subterrania

"WELCOME TO SUBTERRANIA," KAYE SAYS as I step into her room. My eyes take a moment to adjust to the lack of light. I know that outside, a noon sun is in full blaze, that it's a typical Philippine summer, but in here, there is almost no way of telling what the time or season is. Kaye is sitting cross-legged on the carpeted floor, in front of the television. I drop my backpack and plunk myself down beside her. She glances at me, and then she turns her attention back to the TV.

I look around the room. Sketch pads, dog-eared books, coffee-stained notebooks, comics, and video cassettes are scattered everywhere. There's a bed on one side, a small refrigerator right next to it. There's a computer atop a sturdy black desk—its screen saver is active, just three words flowing across a black field: "you are here." In a corner, an airconditioner hums tunelessly to itself. What little light there is comes through slivers and cracks: a broken segment of the window blinds, a lampshade hand-painted in dark swirling patterns. I have this strange sense that we're sitting, not in a room, but inside a sad giant's clasped hands.

She's watching a Japanese animated movie on the VCR. It seems to be about a young cyborg girl with the prerequisite oversized eyes beating up a bunch of massive, shark-faced villains. I don't ask Kaye what it is. She's so engrossed that she might not answer, and then the question would hang in the air, embarassed by its uselessness, by its very existence.

Minutes pass. "This is great," she says, as if suddenly remembering that I'm there. She points at the screen. "Watch how she swings around, and then leaps into the air, how she sets up the death blow." The cartoon figures on the screen dance a violent, slo-mo ballet. The cyborg girl rips through her monstrous opponent. "That guy reminds me of you," Kaye says, and at first I think she means the dead dismembered monster, and then I realize that she's talking about another character, a bespectacled, lanky guy in a trenchcoat— who is, as far as I can tell, friends with the cyborg girl. I'm glad. I guess that means he'll live. We watch the rest of the movie in silence.

As the screen turns blank, Kaye sighs, then stretches, as if waking up. She looks at me.

"Hello there," I say.

She gives me a smile. "Hey," she replies. "So what brings you here?"

"Nothing much," I say. "How are you?"

"Good," she says. "Pretty good…"

"I can't really stay," I tell her. "I just brought that CD you were asking for."

"Hey, great," she says, brightening up a little. I reach into my backpack, fish around until I can feel the flat square case, and hand her the CD. She thanks me, crawls over to where her stereo is, and pops the disc in. I get up. She presses 'play,' I give her a goodbye salute, and as the room fills with the sound of pulsing keyboards, a skitter-scatter electronic beat, and the plaintive, repetitive croon of a sampled female singer, I make my exit.

⊕   ⊕   ⊕

I REMEMBER THE FIRST TIME WE TALKED about Subterannia. We were in Virra Mall, that hobbyist's haven, walking through the dingy corridors of the video-game parlors on the third floor. Row upon row of grubby schoolboys and grubbier twentynothings, their faces lit by the crazily changing colors shed by the game screens. "Life among the morlocks," she said. I laughed, a short laugh that ended as soon as I realized she wasn't making a joke. We walked past more shops, more gaudy machines, more slack sweaty faces. The machines were screaming, roaring, cursing, making laserbeam-sounds and explosion-sounds.

"In a way, there's something wonderful about this," she said.

"What do you mean?" I asked.

"This, I don't know, this separation from reality. These people hunched in front of their virtual playgrounds. They know the rules, they know how to win, and they know exactly who's to blame when they lose. And they don't have to admit other people into their worlds unless they want to."

I didn't know how to reply. The blaring sound effects were beginning to make me feel slightly dizzy. I tugged at her arm and we started walking towards the escalator. "They should rename this part of the mall. Call it Subterrania," I said. From that day on, we used that word to refer to any area that was cut off, that lacked sufficient light or air, that felt like a dark world unto itself.

⊕　　⊕　　⊕

THE NEXT TIME I VISIT HER, she's curled up on the bed, reading a comic book. She looks up when I enter, says, "Hey," and drags herself up to a sitting position on the bed's edge.

"Helfo," I say, pulling up a chair. "The dry season is over, you know. No more hot sun. You can come out now."

"I went out for a few minutes, last night."

"You did?"

"Yeah. Walked around the neighborhood a bit. Saw a fishball vendor, an old lady, some dogs. There's not much out there."

"Well, there's a big concert at the Sunken Garden tomorrow night. You wanna go?"

She shakes her head. "I can see it now. People packed together, lots of sweating and grabbing, lots of pot and cigarette smoke, and a ratio of five lousy bands to every single decent act."

"You used to like going to those concerts."

"I like *this*," she says, gesturing around her.

I make a sound that's not quite a sigh. "Okay."

"Hey," she says, with a reassuring tone to her voice, "Don't worry about me. I've got everything. Food and shelter, reading material and a stereo. I've got an Internet connection. Occasional visits from friends like you. Everything important."

"Okay," I say again, and then I don't know what else to say. Half a minute or so of silence passes. "Oh," I blurt, remembering something, "Here's that book I was telling you about." I reach into my bag.

"Thanks," she says, as she takes the book. I gesture towards the door, and tell her I have to be off. She nods, and I get up, and leave.

She's beginning to worry me.

⊕   ⊕   ⊕

KAYE AND I USED TO GALLIVANT AROUND the metropolis during our spare time. (We had a lot of spare time then, being college students in courses that we considered fairly easy). We found many small Subterranias. There was the underpass at Lawton, with its graffiti, its snack and cigarette vendors, its distinctive smell. The unfinished top floor of our old high school's Humanities building—we went up there once, during a reunion—it was a network of bare, unpainted classrooms, with metal rods and concrete blocks on the floor; that was Subterrania too, even though it was five stories up. And Kaye discovered one day, while waiting for a bus, that a crack in a wall, if you stay still and stare at it long enough, if you can somehow imagine yourself, feel yourself inside it, squeeze your mind into that space — that jagged gap can be Subterrania too.

⊕   ⊕   ⊕

ANOTHER VISIT. IT'S BEEN WEEKS AND WEEKS since Kaye breathed the air outside, or saw the sun or moon, except on TV or through her blinds. I ask her why she doesn't want to leave her room any more. Why her books and CDs and things have become more interesting than the sprawl of the world outside. They always were, she claims, she just hadn't realized it before. "I love these things," she said, "these stories, these songs— because even the worst of them, in their own way, are perfect. Better than a life of uncertainty. They have beginnings and endings. I get the world distilled, you know, in its purer form. Even news stories on CNN have lifespans. They don't cover certain events forever. Everything begins and everything ends, and that's wonderful. You know what's going on when you read a book, when you listen to a song or look at a painting. Or even if you don't know what's going on, you know that there are underlying reasons for everything. All these things are perfect flawed worlds. This room is *my* perfect flawed world…" Once again: I don't know what to say to her.

⊕   ⊕   ⊕

THERE ARE TIMES THESE DAYS, when I'm outside, crossing a busy street, or buying groceries, that I think of Kaye and her room and her world, of Subterrania, and I feel something like sadness, something like intense longing. These moments can hit me at almost any time. Sitting in my apartment, watching an inane sitcom on TV. Paying my bills. Arguing with a traffic cop who just wants a bribe. Sometimes, when I'm just waking up from a dream, I get confused; I don't know which is which, which world is Kaye's world and which world is my world, the world of traffic and noise and aggravation, and at these times, they seem more different and more alike than ever.

⊕ ⊕ ⊕

MONTHS AND MONTHS HAVE PASSED. I can hardly remember what it was like before, when Kaye and I used to go out. "Why do you come here?" she asks. "Are you expecting something from me?" She has these sullen moods once in a while. At other times, she's almost absurdly grateful to see me. She gives me a hug as if I'm her oldest friend in the world—which I will be, if she keeps up this hibernation. But to silently answer her question, a perfectly valid question, a valid concern: I don't expect anything, really. No more than this, anyway.

⊕ ⊕ ⊕

THERE ARE A NUMBER OF WAYS OUR STORY COULD END. (It is *our* story now, I believe, not completely hers and not completely mine. Had I stopped visiting her, I would have been a mere blip on her radar, a cameo appearance in her life-movie. And perhaps, though not inevitably, vice versa. But distinctions have been blurred, lines have been crossed, and we're in this together now. I think).

1. There could be a fire. It doesn't have to be a fire, really; any sort of disaster would do. I can imagine the heat, the sound, I see myself emerging from the flames, Kaye in my arms, her hands clasped behind my neck. I stride across their front yard as the house behind me crackles and sputters. As soon as I reach a spot that's far away enough, I lay Kaye gently down on the grass. She coughs, takes one, two, three deep breaths, and then opens her wet eyes. We look at each other for a long time, for the first time, and her lips part slightly—

2. She never leaves her room. I visit her day after day. Every time I visit her, I feel a little older, a little weaker; but she stays the same, young, immortal.

Years pass. I'm an old man, with a cane, or a wheelchair. She's still in her mid-twenties, her body is still lithe, unwrinkled. I bring her books, music, magazines, myself, day after day after day, until my heart spasms itself into stopping. I fall with a thud on her carpeted floor, in her airconditioned, undisturbed room.

3. She changes. It's slow at first; her skin seems paler, clammier. After a few years her eyes seem strange, like her pupils are smaller, but it's hard to tell what's happening because of the dimness of her room. Slowly her fingers and toes grow sucker-like tips, the better to manipulate her appliances and reading materials with. Her head starts to change shape, it becomes longer, flatter. She starts moving around on all fours. One day I enter her room to find something that isn't recognizably Kaye at all, or even recognizably human. It looks like a giant albino mole, hairless and exuding a sickly-sweet smell. It looks at me, then looks away.

4. My last visit. She asks me what I've brought her. I reach into my bag and pull out a small, dull-black gun. We look at each other and there are no questions.

5. And so on.

⊕   ⊕   ⊕

How many times have I visited her now? How many days has she spent in this room? I've lost count of both values. This is another day, another visit.

I step into the room. She's curled up on the carpeted floor, and for a brief dizzy moment, I think she might be dead, but she's not; I notice the rise and fall of her ribcage, the gentle sound of her breathing. Her stereo is playing something that sounds like pygmies chanting. It is oddly soothing.

"Kaye," I say, more to hear the sound of her name as a kind of counterpoint to the chants than out of any need for a reply. She makes a small kind of *hrmm?* sound in return but doesn't budge. She's wearing an old tank top and loose floral pajama bottoms, having long ago ceased seriously caring about her appearance in front of me. From where I'm standing, I can see her shoulder blades jutting out, and the first bumps of her spinal column.

"Turn off the lamp, please," she says. "But don't leave me."

I turn off the lamp. All is blackness. I kneel down, then settle into a fetal position. I wonder where she is; I can't see a thing. All of a sudden, I feel her breath on my face. She's right in front of me. We lie there together, not touching, not speaking. The sound of chanting fills me, fills my heart; it's the only sound in the world. Slowly, her face seems to form before mine. I can make out the slight curves of her cheekbones, her forehead, her eyes. The thought crosses my mind: it should be impossible to see anything in darkness this total. Anything at all.

Louise Welsh

Young Lochinvar

ROBERT SHOT HIS FIRST FAMILY AT TEN O'CLOCK THAT MORNING. He told them where to stand, whispering instructions in a soft voice he meant to be soothing, then put his eye to the viewfinder, fixed all six in the crosshatch of his sights and captured them in a flash of light just as the father bent his mouth into a grin that would make a gargoyle weep. Robert sighed, reloaded and prepared to start again. It was going to be another long day.

One of the *National Geographic* magazines that lay curling on the waiting room table of Mr. Giaconelli's Gorbals studio, contained an article about an aboriginal tribe who thought photographers stole people's spirits. The cover featured a Technicolor shot of elders, caught leaping from drowsy gossip into panic, half hidden features caught in terror, hands thrown up, fingers splayed, shielding their faces in a desperate bid to save their souls. When Robert reviewed the blank expressions in the formal portraits that comprised the stock of his trade, he thought the aboriginals didn't go far enough. The camera didn't stop at the subject's souls, it sapped the photographer's as well.

The day dragged to its close and at six o'clock Robert turned the sign on the front door from *We Are Open for Kodak Film* to *Closed, We Will Be Open for Kodak Film Tomorrow* which, as the next day was Sunday, wasn't at all accurate. He started setting the front shop to rights then stopped. It was as if he could feel someone looking at him. Robert slowly turned and looked up. Gleaming from a high shelf of the display cabinet was his boss's tiptop, brand new zoom lens. Robert slid back the glass, took the lens in his hands and rolled it between his palms, admiring its lightness. There was no way Mr. G would ever let him use such an expensive piece of equipment, but with its help the right photographer could become a genius. The thought had no sooner entered his head than the door studio opened and Robert quickly shoved the lens into his pocket.

'So what does the morrow hold for this bold boy?'

Twenty years ago, newly arrived in Scotland, Mr. Giaconelli had turned to the romances of Sir Walter Scott in an attempt to improve his English. The result was a mix of Italian, Glaswegian and medievalism, which along with his Valentino looks had won him the heart and hand of Janice Connelly, a happy union resulting in five boys and the darling of the brood, sixteen-year-old Marie.

Robert looked through the gap between the adverts that decorated the glass door and out onto the rain-splattered streets.

'I was thinking of going for a bike ride.'

'Ach it's good to get out in the hills, eh?' Mr. Giaconelli unfastened his dustcoat and began to get into his suit jacket. 'And maybe you'll meet a lassie on the way?' He turned towards the mirror applying a touch of Brylcreem to the dark hair that could still work magic on Janice Giaconelli nee Connelly and started to recite in a voice that almost lilted into song, 'O, young Lochinvar has come out of the west, Through all the wide border his steed was the best; And save his good broadsword he weapon had none, He rode all unarmed, he rode all alone.' Mr. Giaconelli turned towards Robert holding his arms out like Enrico Caruso and finished with a flourish, 'So faithful in love, and so dauntless in war, There never was a knight like the young Lochinvar.'

Robert was used to this. Young Lochinvar was a favourite recitation of Mr. Giaconelli's, though any connection between the hero's antics and his own dull life escaped Robert. He sighed and shrugged on his coat.

'Aye, well if I'm not in Monday morn you'll know what's happened.'

Mr. Giaconelli had worries of his own, but he knew what it was like to be young and alone. He fished the shop keys from his pocket and shook his finger at his assistant.

'For the unmarried swain damsels are a pleasure strictly confined to the weekend. In the meantime, let me buy you a drink. It's Saturday night, eh?'

'Aye, I mean aye it is, but no I'll not stop for a pint thanks.'

As Mr. Giaconelli later said to the peerless Janice over drinks in *The Merry Man*, for a young chap Robert could be, 'A right bloody misery.'

Still, perhaps it was better that he and Janice were alone. Mr. Giaconelli needed to discuss Marie. The light of his life who, though a little headstrong, had never given any trouble until she'd left school for teacher training college. There she'd met young Alec Lenzie, beatnik and general waster and suddenly sweet Marie had changed. Only the previous night his daughter had stayed out until ten thirty. When she'd eventually come home Mr. Giaconelli had noticed an oil stain on her coat which could mean only one thing—a motorbike.

Janice leaned into him and took a sip of her port and lemon.

'Marie's not daft Angelo, she'll soon get bored with Alec.' She gave him a warning look. 'Unless you turn him into Marlon Brando by telling her what an outlaw he is.'

Mr. Giaconelli wasn't convinced. Like most fathers who remember their own youth, he distrusted young men. He raised his brown eyes to Janice.

'If she needs a suitor why not a steady chap like young Robert?'

Janice squeezed his hand. 'It's as well you've got me to look after you. Anyway, you'll be glad to hear that for the first Saturday night in a long while your daughter is forswearing the dancing to keep her old mother and dad company. So come on, drink up and I'll make us all dinner.'

Mr. Giaconelli returned Janice's squeeze. But as he finished his pint he made a vow. Anyone who messed with his little girl would have him and his five strong sons to reckon with.

WHILE THE GIACONELLIS RELAXED, Robert walked the three streets to his lodgings cultivating fine feelings of angst and wishing to God he were in Paris. The Gorbals' slums were being torn down, the residents relocated. Soon there would be a new world, but right now the district was a ghostly maze of half abandoned streets punctuated by desolate gap sites reminiscent of the bomb craters he'd played in as a boy. Robert took off his cap and bared his head to the rain. He was at one with the fractured landscape, the empty streets and soot black buildings. This was the cusp of time, caught between the half demolished past and an unknown future. Already he felt nostalgia for a life not yet done. Robert took out his camera and captured rain-varnished cobbles shining between two rows of glowering tenements.

Robert lived in an abandoned flat, a 'single end' at the top of a tenement block earmarked for demolition. He climbed the dark ammonia-scented stairwell, whistling a French song about falling leaves and a lover who left in the autumn. Inside, Robert's home was unexpectedly cosy. One room equipped with an Ulster sink, temperamental range, bed recess draped with curtains, a small table and two upright chairs. The flat saw no visitors and the redundant chair was stacked with back copies of *The Picture Post*. Robert flicked through the latest issue until he reached the image of a looming mountain, ink black against the grainy grey of the sky. He wondered if the photographers hallowed in these pages had ever been forced to take family photographs. Somehow he doubted it.

Robert had draped the lone window above the sink with some old blackout material he'd found at Paddy's market and lined the gas mantles with red cellophane turning the tiny apartment into one big photographic darkroom. The fruits of the darkroom hung, pinned along lengths of cotton strung from the drying pulley, dozens of photographs, his real work. The young photographer lowered his gallery and unpegged a print taken only the previous evening.

A man in a slouch cap and vest leant out of a tenement window smoking a cigarette, taking the air. His eyes were hidden in the shadows, but the weary end of the day was etched behind wisps of smoke on the down-turned cast of his exhaling mouth. The man's face was a picture of melancholy. It seemed like this last air, filtered through tobacco at dusk, was his only taste of freedom.

He reached for another photograph. A man and woman embraced at the mouth of an alley. His dark suit pressed hard against her fawn coat, her arms clenched into his back, his work boots sandwiched between her stilettos, her hands linked into a bond the man had no wish to break. The darkness of the doorway held them shadowless against the black.

Robert cringed as he looked at the image. The dark had forced him to use a flash and the couple had broken their clinch, passion as equal in their fury as it had been in the kiss. Robert had made a run for it, pulling his own hat low over his ears, hoping to God the man hadn't recognised him.

Still, there was nothing to be ashamed of Robert reasoned. He was as much an anthropologist as the man from the *National Geographic*. Wasn't he recording a vanishing world? The subjects might be resistant, but like the journalist faced with the superstitious aboriginals he would persist, no matter the danger.

Robert brewed himself a mug of tea, topped it up with a tot of whisky and checked his watch, time to get started. He lowered the lights, slipped his camera from its hiding place beneath the pillow and screwed on the borrowed zoom, then unfolded his shortest tripod onto the coal bunker, set the camera upon it and shifted the blackout material a peep.

Opposite, through the darkness, in a sliver of light between curtains that almost met, Jean Gow sat at her dressing table stroking a hairbrush through curls as red and soft waved as Maureen O'Hara's. She lowered the brush and reached towards something beyond Robert's sight. He held his breath and clicked just as eye, lip, curls, high curve of the cheek slipped into view. The woman leant back again and he was left with a tantalising glimpse of her profile. Jean was powdering her face, as intent on the image in the mirror as Robert was in the vision through his camera lens. He waited till she lowered the pink powder puff to the hollow of her bosom and clicked once more, recording the wonder of flesh that would one day wrinkle and change. Robert shifted in his seat as Jean dropped her raylon dressing gown, revealing a glimpse of peach satin bra and cami-knickers that he caught with a snap of the shutter. Robert was so deep in anticipation of Jean's next move that he didn't hear the scuff of feet on the stair outside, nor the turn of the handle, or the asthmatic creak of the door to his apartment. The visitor was three steps into the room before Robert jumped to his feet.

Before him stood a young bohemian of the type that would never grace his studio. A young woman dressed in a ratty navy skirt, tight blue and white-hooped jumper topped by an old suede jacket and black beret. Robert's mouth opened into a perfect O. It wasn't until she said,

'Dad asked me to invite you round for dinner.'

That Robert recognised Marie Giaconelli, the girl he'd last seen neatly turned out in a school uniform and the source of all Mr. Giaconelli's sorrows. Marie pushed a strand of wet hair away from her eyes. Her cheeks were pink from the cold and the climb. She looked at the camera and asked,

'What are you doing?'

Robert covered the camera's lens, stuttering,

'A wee personal project . . . a study of the night sky . . .' then, remembering another *National Geographic* article, 'a constellation that only comes into alignment at this time of the year.'

Later it occurred to Robert that he should have invented a less interesting excuse, something that wouldn't have brought Marie Giaconelli to the sink where she edged him aside, resting her hip where it had no business to be and putting an eye to the lens. She looked in silence for a second then said in a voice heavy with wonder,

'You dirty bugger. That's Jean Gow in her scanties.'

'Ach you budged the camera when you shoved in.'

'So that it was perfectly focused on the gap in the curtain just as she's doing the nudie fandango?'

'She's not is she?'

Marie pushed the camera aside. 'It wouldn't surprise me if she knew you were watching. Nobody wears lingerie like that if they don't want it seen. Honestly you're as bad as my brothers.' The girl looked around exploring the small space. 'I've never been in your flat before.'

'That's because you've never been invited.'

Marie ignored the slight.

'You're lucky having a place of your own. We're all squashed together up the road.' She lifted Robert's Saturday night quarter bottle of whisky from the mantle shelf, unscrewed the top and took a swig. 'No room to breathe.' She let her gaze linger on the curtains veiling the bed recess, then turned abruptly to the pulley cord, lowering the cache of photographs. Robert moved to stop her, but living with five brothers had taught Marie to look lively and she'd unpegged a print before the young photographer was even halfway across the room.

Robert had captured many fine images, reflections of a vanishing world. There were only a few guilty glimpses of Jean Gow stripping, and those hidden at the back of the collection. Marie lighted on them with the instinct of a hanging judge.

'Will the depravity never end?' She scrutinised a shot with an expression of scorn that in years to come would silence generations of school children. 'You're a sad case Robert. Imagine turning Peeping Tom for that.'

'It's the human form, nothing to be ashamed of.'

'So you'll be dropping round with a few copies for her man?'

Jean Gow's husband was known in bars and bare knuckle boxing booths throughout the East End.

'I don't think Raymond Gow's got the temperament to appreciate artistic endeavour.'

Marie took another swig of whisky. 'I don't imagine many men do when it involves sneaky shots of their naked wife.'

Suddenly the uselessness of it all descended on Robert.

'I want to be an artist Marie, I don't want to be confined to taking portraits of ba'faced weans and throttle-necked grannies in your dad's studio. Okay, I shouldn't have photographed Jean without permission, but artists need artistic subjects and what could be more artistic than Jean Gow?'

Marie swigged thoughtfully from the bottle.

'I'm not convinced you're not just a randy wee radge on the make. But if you promise to make it artistic then I'll do it for you.'

'Do what?'

'Model. Surely I'd do as well as Jean Gow?'

Robert's voice shook a little.

'Are you not headed to the dancing? I wouldn't like to keep you back.'

'No,' Jean hauled her jumper over her head to reveal a slightly grubby vest. 'I've fallen out with Alec,' She unfastened the safety pin at the side of her skirt. 'To be honest I wasn't that struck on him anyway.' She wriggled free and unclipped her brassiere. 'Anyway, the dad's awful queer the now.'

Robert picked up Marie's jumper and handed it to her.

'Speaking of your dad…'

'Aye,' Marie threw it onto a chair. 'I don't know what it is with fathers, but as soon as daughters show any sign of independence they get awful possessive.' She smiled at Robert as she kicked off her shoes. 'And I guess with my dad coming from Italy he's even more old-fashioned than the rest.' She laughed, unfastened her woollen stockings and let them fall to the floor. 'I reckon that's the reason I kept up with Alec, to show dad he couldn't boss me around.'

'I think he might be angry if he saw you now.'

'Ach dad's a sweet old thing really, for all that he threatened to batter Alec.'

'Speaking of battering, what would your brothers say?'

Marie laughed again and whisky and sweetness were in her laugh,

'Maybe that's the real reason I stayed with Alec, the hope that he'd get a thumping. Anyway, I decided I should stay in the night to make it up to dad. Give him a break from worrying about my honour.' She pulled her knickers down. 'You know we'd best be quick in case he gets anxious.' She put her hands on her hips standing there in nothing but her glory. 'Now, how would you like me to pose?'

Robert had never thought of Marie Giaconelli as anything other than his boss's irritating daughter, but now that she stood stripped before him he could see the raw power of her thighs, the strength in her arms, the smoothness of her olive skin and retroussé breasts. He stifled a groan and averted his gaze to the floor.

'Marie, I think you should put your clothes back on. I'm not sure the education authority would be keen on employing a school teacher who's posed nude.'

She stuck her hips out and asked, 'Ach, how would they ever know?'

'It's only art if I exhibit them. If I take nude photos of you and keep them for my own use, well . . .' he let the sentence tail off.

The young woman sighed. It was a good career, but she feared that this was only the start of the restraints teaching would impose. She picked up the pair of knickers and held them to her. 'I guess you're right.' She looked beyond Robert, out of the window and into the night sky. 'So are you coming to dinner or not?'

Robert put his eye to the camera. The window opposite was in darkness, Jean Gow off to the dancing with her Raymond.

'Aye, may as well I suppose. Just let me put this away.'

Robert was unscrewing the zoom and Marie half into her panties when the knock came at the door. They leapt into action, but neither was a seasoned adulterer. Marie dived naked into the bed recess and Robert threw her clothes out of reach into a trunk beneath the bed. He smoothed the curtains behind her, shouting 'Who's there?' towards the door though, he knew the answer as well as you and I.

'It's me.' Mr. Giaconelli's voice sounded clear and anxious from the lobby.

'Come on in, the door's open.' Robert tried to make his own tones sound natural, but it was only worry that stopped Mr. Giaconelli from spotting his apprentice's distress. The older photographer bustled in.

'Have you seen Marie? I sent her to ask you for dinner. Janice thought you might like some home cooking, she thinks it's lonely, a boy like you sitting alone on a Saturday with no family. But now, an hour later and no sign of Marie or of you so I reckon she's gone out with that waster, the beatnik Alec and now I get here and see she's not arrived so it must be true.'

Robert cupped his hand around the purloined zoom, wishing he hadn't taken it and trying not to look towards the flapping curtain on the bed recess where Marie struggled with a dose of the giggles.

'No it's fine, she was here a minute ago, I think she ran a message for someone on the way, you know how obliging she is.'

Mr. Giaconelli blustered through his relief, 'Aye too obliging, that's what worries me.'

He went to seat himself on the bed.

'Aye, well she's away home now.'

Robert steered Mr. Giaconelli towards a chair. The old man smiled to think how nervous the youth was at having his boss in his simple home.

'Ach, she's a good lassie, clever too. She'll make a fine teacher, a fine wife for some lucky man.' The curtain behind him wavered. Mr. Giaconelli continued blithely. 'I ken she's bossy, but that can be good in a wife.' He laughed. 'Look at me, I married a beesum and never regretted it.'

Robert realised the drift of his boss's talk, and with it the reason for his invitation to dinner. He held up his hand.

'She's an admirable girl, a very good-looking girl, but I'm not really the marrying kind. If I were to marry I'm sure I couldn't do better...'

Robert continued, his excuses becoming falteringly elaborate, but Mr. Giaconelli had ceased to regard him as husband material. He pointed to the purloined zoom lens in Robert's hand.

'You thieving wee bastard!' Outrage gave wings to his rage and with a cry of, 'What more of my property have you hidden here?' Mr. Giaconelli tore back the curtains around the bed recess to reveal his naked daughter.

IT IS A LONG ROAD FROM GLASGOW TO PARIS, especially for a boy with a black eye and no money, but Robert had the promises of the Giaconelli brothers to spur his flight. He'd pawned his camera, left his photographs in a flat marked for demolition and, beyond his ferry fare, was destitute. But Robert had one advantage; he was young enough to find his plight romantic. It was a dreich dark day when he eventually watched the shores of home recede into the distance. He stood on the ferry's deck feeling the salt spray of freedom on his face, and shouted into the wind,

So daring in love and so dauntless in war.

Have you e'er heard of a gallant like young Lochinvar?

ALFRED A. YUSON

Old Shoes

CRUNCH, CRUNCH.

The shoes still feel good on hard ground. After all these years, they've remained warm and protective, a soft, perfect fit.

Well, never had many chances to wear them out, anyway. The shoes are for extremely cold weather, especially when snow is on the ground. No snow here now, not yet, not on this near barren, sodden field, did they call it a lea or a fen, here in Midlothian in Scotland.

Crunch, crunch.

I trudge across the field in Lasswade, heading to the town center from Hawthornden Castle. A similar experience comes back to mind: 14 years previous—1978 in Iowa City, Midwest, USA.

Crunch, crunch.

I trudged with the same pair of shoes—my winter shoes, I called them—on a near barren, sodden field with frozen dewdrops on the ground.

Trudged alongside the Iowa River that snaked through the university campus. Go Hawks! Broke off from the serpentine crystal and crossed the field on a diagonal course toward a red-brick school building, delirious, with a fresh note fluttering in my gloved hand.

Crunch, crunch.

The shoes felt good then, though barely broken. Indian summer had given way to end-September cold. I had just bought the shoes from K-Mart

—dark brown leather but rough-and-tough-looking, with one-inch-thick soles. Made in South Korea. Special feature, said the red tag: a steel sheet was inside those soles. Piscean feet would have metal protection from bitter cold.

'Twas the heart vulnerable, anyway, that day of days. Or loins. That fluttering note, I wanted to wave it against wind-chill factor. I would brandish it before Admin staff in that red-brick building drawing near. I would say: Here's a notice just handed me at the lobby of the Mayflower, it says there's a telegram for me from Manila.

Maila's coming, Maila's coming. Must be it.

They'd say, yes, here's the wire, got in a couple of hours ago, we rang up Mayflower.

'Yes, thanks. I wasn't in my room. Observing the squirrels, over breakfast of burrito and coffee from the Vendo, trying to sun my tropical self on the park bench across the street, by the river. Got the notice only when I crossed back to Mayflower.'

Pilgrim, pilgrim. Will Maila land beside you soon?

Hope it's good news, sir.

Tear up the tear sheet. Darned staple. Fingers trembling, gloveless now inside red-brick lobby.

Yes! Oh yes! Maila got her leave. We fuck again by second week of October. The 9th, she's getting here on the 9th. October light. Why, that's Da Vinci's birthday. Heh-heh, turn ambidextrous that night, both hands on her teats. Sheee-it, as they say here, been on a drought for six weeks. She too, I suppose. But she won't be dry on Leonardo's b-day.

'Yes! Good news indeed, ma'am. My honeypot's joining me here for a month.'

Oh, good to hear that, sir. Coming all the way from Manila is she?

'Yup. Yeah, my darling Maila is.'

Well, good for you, sir. Have a good day. Have a good month.

Crunch, crunch.

Trudge back across that diagonal path, across that same field lined by a bit of color change: birch, poplar, aspen—trees unfamiliar to eyes tropical, yet elegant, stately.

The shoes feel good. Thank you, Kim and Kim and Kim. I can still jump and do a half-twirl, delirious over the news: lonely bed soon to be relieved by October light.

MID-APRIL IN MIDLOTHIAN. Snow flurry now and then, still.

In Edinburgh, snowflakes whipped about one afternoon, settling gently round my shoulders. I celebrated with a bottle of Lagavulin.

1992. I imagine: the young J.K. Rowling nursing cups of coffee on the second floor of Burger King, is it, where I sometimes come for silent company, the view of Castle Rock across Princes Street.

Too quiet in Drummond's castle. Days of poems by the small room's fireplace, a sandwich and tea found in the hallway at noon sharp. No voice to trade with on long hours, long days.

Excuse me, silent spirits, let me ease myself out, crunch crunch through the gravel path, crows murdering the large trees, caw-cawing overhead as I make it to the empty road, where I wait minutes for the bus.

Must have missed the last one, barely. I get impatient and walk up the macadam. The town center looks close, beyond a curve. I cross the lea or fen.

Crunch crunch toward Lasswade.

Iowa comes back to mind. Maila arrives and spends a month with me at Mayflower Apartments. We are hungry for one another, and boy, do we make out the first night, the second day, etc. The International Writing Program is no more than a circus, I explain to her. No need for my presence in any activity; it's a long-drawn party. And Maila's accepted by everyone as yet another

Significant Other who's followed her mate or lover, just like the Singaporean couple, or the Kenyan, or the German. The Indian fellow brought in a family, and when Maila and I walk through the hallway on the Mayflower's 4th floor, we can smell fragrant curry from their kitchen. And while waiting for the elevator we laugh and kiss and hurriedly turn back and make out in my room, where the narrow beds often groan under our wild play, and I lift her up and we hurtle across the room toward the window with a front view, and I lay her rump against the console with the TV set, and thrust into her gasping while eyeing the river beyond her hair, down there, across the street, imagine the squirrels scurrying under birch, poplar, aspen…

Crunch crunch toward Lasswade.

Imelda Romualdez Marcos comes to mind, how she spent our country's money on thousands of shoes, I'd like her face under my own, here on the hard cold ground, ground her puffy cheeks with my Made in Korea winter shoes.

Maila fondles the dark brown pair, holds them up against October light in our Mayflower room. Nifty, she says. Steel inside, you say? 'So Kim & Kim & Kim claim,' I say. 'They're warm even on cold hard ground. Make my feet so warm, as warm as you pussy-babe.' Maila tosses them over her shoulder and one hits the TV set with a plink that I imagine to come from the metal sheet inside its sole. And Maila pushes me back to bed and grabs my feet and hold them high against October light, kisses my soles, licks up to toes she bites and sucks, then thrusts one big one down toward her crotch. Here, warm it up, boy, let's warm it up inside me, Pisces Boy. Oh, Maila Maila.

Crunch crunch toward Lasswade.

I get to the street. Cross over to what looks like a pub, right by a bus stop. I push a door open and squint hard at the dark interior, make out some figures, old men huddled around a table or two. They all turn and check out the arrival. Their faces are impassive. Some even seem to turn surly upon their inspection of who-this-guy, some Chink or Jap, or is he Mexican? No one says a word and I hang there still, poised and tensing between street of early-Spring light and the pub's gloomy, smoky cast.

I backtrack and swivel slowly round on the pavement, the shoes making a swishing sound, no plink. Downright unfriendly, I say to myself. Maybe they quickly surmised I was yet another out-of-towner from the castle, a foreigner, even, Asian. But if someone had said hello, welcome, sit yourself, lad, they might have gotten to know I came from Manila, and they'd say, oh, Imelda, yes, we've heard of her, thousands of shoes, right, laddie? She takes the high road, we take the low road…

The bus comes, and I hop in, one of the dozen-year-old shoes going plink as it scrapes across the jumpstep, metal on metal.

I think of Imelda, Maila, Malinda of Iowa when Maila left in November, how we started getting it on somewhat in that dim bar called Sanctuary, but when we went to her place warming up toward each other, my new shoes shuffling softly on Malinda's doorstep, we're surprised 'cause a man's voice sounds out from inside, and it turns out her boyfriend's back from Des Moines for the weekend. There goes Malinda, the chance to cast off those shoes by Kim & Co. right in her bedroom.

I think of Malinda, Maila and Imelda all through the hour's ride to Edinburgh.

A WHOLE AFTERNOON TO WASTE before the last bus back to Hawthornden. I've had my fill of Castle Rock, the Museum of Whisky, Camera Obscura. This time I turn right on Royal Mile and wander about till I see a sign saying Scottish Poetry Library, pointing to an alley cum cul-de-sac: 5 Crichton's Close, Canongate.

Hello, good afternoon, Ma'am, I say to the old lady by the welcome desk. She's friendly and asks me to register if I want to, which I do, thence browse around, and finally ask her for a book by Drummond, William.

"That she thy career may with roses spread;/ The nightingales thy coming each-where sing;/ Make an eternal spring;/ Give life to this dark world which lieth dead./ Spread forth thy golden hair/ In larger locks than thou wast wont before,.../

"...Night like a drunkard reels/ Beyond the hills to shun his flaming wheels..."

Hmm. Crunch, crunch.

I amble off in the direction of Arthur's Seat, notice a small crowd gathering before a small art gallery. Why, it's newly opened, with but a dozen well-dressed ladies and gentlemen making their way inside. Approaching the large glass pane, I peer at the works—colorful paintings in large, simply framed canvases. I notice a small poster taped to the glass.

Someone by the doorway waves to catch my eye. I look up from the text announcing an exciting debut by a male artist, and smile pleasantly at the fetching lady waving me to come in.

Do join us, she chirps enticingly. You'll have a better view of the works inside. They're exciting.

'Is that right?' I respond chirpingly, and turn toward her. Chiffon, summer dress, floral prints, shapely alabaster legs.

Do come in. I'm Chantal, and I curated the exhibit.

'Hello, Chantal. *Enchanté* to meet you. This your gallery?'

No, just guest curating, regular fellow's a friend of mine, but he fell ill. Oh, not serious at all. Bollocks type. And so is the artist a friend of mine. He's very good. Very exciting. Here, have some wine. We only have red.

"Why, thank you, Chantal. Here's to red sails in the sunset.'

Hmm. You visiting Edinburgh? Why, that's a poetry book under your arm.

'Yes, yes. Just stopped by the Poetry Library. Staying at Hawthornden, the International Retreat for Writers.'

Oh, bonnie! I knew it, when I called you in, you'd be special. Must be those shoes, they're a holdover from winter, right? And no winter where you come from.

Chantal was like that, she leapt out of bed the way she did at conversation, with a frolicking manner, spreading forth her golden hair.

"The Graces naked danced about the place," I had read to her that night, and she bared herself before doing me, while I read on from the library book.

"…The winds and trees amazed/ With silence on her gazed,/ The flowers did smile, like those upon her face;/ And as their aspen stalks those fingers band,/ That she might read my case. / A hyacinth I wish'd me in her hand."

In her hand was my Oriental thing, while the pale fingers of the other tugged at the tight laces of my old shoes. Plink. Plink. They flew away across her cold room. No fireplace. But our heat together was enough for an hour, two, the second spent under her quilt, or having to pad quickly to her small kitchen to retrieve the coffee she brewed, or the bottle of cheap Teacher's, both after a while, and yet my feet grew cold, colder and colder whenever out of the sheets.

On my last trip back to the bed I picked up my shoes and plunked my cold feet in, handed Chantal her cup of steaming coffee, raised my Scotch glass, until she pulled me in again across her. I poked and fingered, mounted, and inserted, and her cold pink fingers grabbed my buttocks and clawed.

Then she freaked when her big toes felt my old shoes. She pushed me back, away, sitting bolt upright, aghast. She stared down at the dark brown shoes, and nearly shrieked. I was laughing when she ordered me out of her room, couldn't believe it. She couldn't believe it. I couldn't believe it.

Our faith together was short. I scrambled to gather my laces and pants and shirt and sweater and jacket and cap and gloves, the book of poems by William Drummond of Hawthornden. Because I could not believe she was shrieking what she was shrieking, so that soon I saw myself in a movie, jaded corny scene, out in a corridor stuffing myself into cold clothes, shivering but stumbling down some dark stairs and out the door into the cold cold street.

Crunch, crunch.

Cursing. I was cursing.

Imelda's got nothing on me, ya hear. Nothing. Nothing!

Glossary of Pinoy Terms

"Alam mo" – you know

Ayan – there

"Bata pa, baldado na!" – Still young, but already defective/crippled/disabled!

Adobo – Chicken and/or pork sautéed in soy sauce, vinegar and garlic and pepper

Anit – scalp

Barkada – group of friends, clique

'Eto – contraction of *heto*: here

"Ewan ko ba" – I don't know

Galis – Sarna infection

GRO – Guest Relations Officer, usually meaning a "bargirl" or prostitute

Ingrata – Ingrate (from Spanish)

Kamusta – popular form of *kumusta:* "how are you?" (from Spanish *Como esta?)*

Kano – American or Caucasian (from "Ameri*kano")*

Kubo – "nipa hut" or native dwelling, usually made of bamboo and coconut

Lawanit – low-cost wall paneling processed from coconut fibers

Lolo – grandfather

Mahina – weak, inferior

Manong – "mister"

Masa – "the masses," also used as an adjective

Pinoy – Filipino

Puta! – bitch!

Retrobada – one who answers back (from Spanish)

Salamat – thank you

Simberguensa – without shame (from Spanish *sin verguenza*)

Talaga – really?

Tikbalang – Filipino counterpart to the centaur (but scarier)

Tita – Auntie

Tricycle – form of public transport in the Philippines, a motorcycle with a sidecar attached for passengers

THE EDITORS

Toni Davidson's debut novel *Scar Culture* [Canongate/Rebel Inc., 2000] has been published in 11 countries, optioned for a TV mini-series by SMG and influenced the name-change of a death metal band from Brooklyn, NY. He has edited two previous anthologies *And Thus Will I Freely Sing* [Polygon, 1989] and *Intoxication: an anthology of stimulant based writing* [Serpent's Tail, 1998]. He has performed his work at Rebel Inc. and Flow events in Scotland, the Edinburgh Book Festival, British Council organised events in Germany and the Philippines, Crossing Border Festival in Holland, Humboldt University in California, The Distilled Festival in New York, the Harbourfront Reading Series (Canada) and at the CCA (Glasgow, Scotland).

Angelo R Lacuesta has received several national awards in the Philippines for his fiction, including the Madrigal-Gonzalez Best First Book Award and the National Book Award for his first book, *Life Before X and Other Stories* [University of the Philippines Press. 2000] His second collection of short fiction, *White Elephants: Stories*, was recently published by Anvil Publishing. He has co-edited, with Jose Y. Dalisay, a previous anthology, *Fourteen Love Stories* [University of the Philippines Press, 2004]. He has participated in various local and international writing programs, among them a writing fellowship at the Hawthornden International Retreat for Writers in Lasswade, Scotland.

THE WRITERS

Dean Francis Alfar is an award-winning playwright, speculative fictionist and comic book creator. His recent works include *Siglo: Freedom* [Nautilus, 2004], a collection of short historical vignettes in comic book form; and "L'Aquilone du Estrellas (The Kite of Stars)," published in *The Year's Best Fantasy & Horror Seventeenth Annual Collection* [St. Martin's Press, 2004]. Between the demands of his marketing company and his pet store, he engages in guerrilla writing and polishing his first novel.

Graham Bell is currently living in Spain writing bilingual rock songs with his group Los TrasTornaos. Rumoured to have connections with deposed Russian aristocrat Le Comptessa. Published stories, various pamphlets and woo manifestos and a shopping list (New Writing Scotland 10). Born in Aberdeenshire the only song which mentions his home town is "The Quine that did the Strip at Inverurie" advice which he has followed in his performing career. A sophisticated primitive, his interest in transgender has flowered in his films *us-in-the-future* and *Choose Your Godless*.

Jose Y. Dalisay has published eleven books of fiction and non-fiction, and teaches English and creative writing at the University of the Philippines. He was a Hawthornden fellow in 1994, and it was in Scotland where he completed *Penmanship and Other Stories* [Cacho Publishing House, Manila, 1995], to which "We Global Men" belongs.

Maria L. M. Fres-Felix is a guerrilla writer, snatching the opportunity to write at odd times and places. She scribbles on the back of old receipts and "writes in her head" while driving to and from her full-time job as a Vice President for a government-owned corporation. She has written two books: *Sup?* which won the Grand Prize for the Pilar Perez Medallion for Teen Literature, and was a finalist for the National Book Award, and *Making Straight Circles*, a story collection. Fres-Felix earned her Masters Degree in Development Economics from Williams College in Massachusetts. She lives in Quezon City with husband Christopher, daughter Kathleen Marie, and labrador retriever, Enzo.

Luis Joaquin M. Katigbak has won several Palanca and Philippine Graphic awards for his fiction. His collection of short stories, *Happy Endings* [University of the Philippines Press, 2000], is now in its fourth printing. He has also written an enormous amount of features and reviews for broadsheets and magazines, scripts for MTV Philippines, and drivel for the consumption of his closest and most unfortunate friends. He is currently working on a second book, his karma, and his weight.

Originally from Aberdeen, Scotland, Iain Maloney graduated from Glasgow University's Creative Writing MPhil in 2004 and is currently putting the finishing touches to his first novel, *Sometimes Sleep*. He has had both poetry and prose published in various magazines and collections including *Stramash*, an anthology of work from the 2003/4 MPhil intake. In 1999 he self-published a book of poetry, *Fences We Build*, which is still available in various bookshop bargain bins around Scotland.

Menchu Aquino Sarmiento trained as a visual artist and runs a non-profit charity in Manila. Her essays and fiction have won Philippine awards. Her short stories are collected in *Daisy Nueve* [Anvil Publishing, Manila, 2003]. Filipino readers have accused her of being cruel to her characters. She is pleased that they care so much about them, but reminds these gentle souls, that they are her characters and she can do with them whatever she pleases.

Adrian Searle lives in Glasgow with his partner and two children and works in graphic design. He edited *The Hope That Kills Us: An Anthology of Scottish Football Fiction* [Polygon, 2003], and published *The Knuckle End* [Freight, 2004], an anthology featuring writers from the University of Glasgow's Creative Writing MPhil programme.

Lakambini A. Sitoy was David TK Wong Fellow at the University of East Anglia, Norwich, United Kingdom in 2003. She has won numerous national-level awards for her fiction in the Philippines, including six Don Carlos Palanca Memorial Awards and a National Book Award. Her stories have appeared in magazines and anthologies in her home country and abroad, *MANOA: A Pacific Journal of International Writing*, published by the University of Hawaii. *Jungle Planet*, her second collection of fiction, following 1998's *Mens Rea,* was published in 2005. Sitoy has worked as an editor, teacher and columnist. She paints in her spare time.

Zoë Strachan was born in 1975 and grew up in Kilmarnock. She gained an MLitt in Creative Writing from the Universities of Glasgow and Strathclyde and her first novel, *Negative Space* [Picador], was published in 2002. It won a Betty Trask Award and was shortlisted for the Saltire First Book of the Year Award. In 2004 she received a Hawthornden Fellowship, and her second novel, *Spin Cycle* [Picador], came out last August. She has published short stories in literary magazines as well as extensive newspaper journalism, and written for radio. She teaches on the MPhil in Creative Writing at Glasgow University.

Mark Waddell's contribution is an excerpt from his first novel *Lizard Luck*. The text has been performed with a soundtrack at the Edinburgh International Book Festival and the Cobden Club, London. He has contributed fiction to an eclectic range of publications and is currently working on a new novel about a suicide club that goes wrong. In the Summer of 1999 he took part as a creative writer in 'Syzygy,' a unique arts/science experiment on a remote Scottish Island, exploring parallels between the way ideas and weather are formed. Born with a sense of humour and a passion for ideas, he believes in the transformative power of the imagination. Recently moved from Glasgow to London, he has discovered the streets are paved with people, not gold.

Until recently **Louise Welsh** was a dealer in secondhand books. Her first novel, *The Cutting Room* is being translated into eighteen languages, was awarded the John Creasey Memorial Dagger, the Corine International first book prize (Germany) and shared The Saltire First Book Award. It was also nominated for the Orange Prize and is included in the Stonewall Honor Book (US). *The Guardian* chose Louise as one of Britain's Best First Novelists of 2002 and a woman to watch, in 2003. Louise was granted a Robert Louis Stevenson Memorial Award in 2003 and a Glenfiddich Spirit of Scotland Award in 2004. She is a regular radio broadcaster, has published many short stories and contributed articles and reviews to most of the British broadsheets. Her second book, *Tamburlaine Must Die*, a novelette written around the final three days of Christopher Marlowe's life, was published to critical acclaim in August 2004. Louise lives in Glasgow.

Mela Vich prefers to give little information due to exceptional and traumatic circumstances. She has lived most of her life on the move across Europe and the USA. She is not yet standing still.

Alfred A. Yuson has authored nineteen books thus far: poetry, short story and essay collections, novels, children's stories, biography, translation, and travel. He has received numerous national and international distinctions, including the SEAWrite (SouthEast Asia Writers) Award given by Thai royalty in Bangkok, and a Rockefeller Foundation fellowship at the Bellagio Center in Italy. In the Philippines, he has been elevated to the Hall of Fame of the Carlos Palanca Memorial Awards for Literature. His work has been translated into Bahasa, Chinese, Japanese, Spanish, French, Italian, Dutch and Norwegian. He has participated in various international literary festivals, the most recent having been the Poetry International 2004 in Rotterdam, The Netherlands, and Poetry Africa 2005 in Dunbar, South Africa. In 1992 he enjoyed a fellowship at the international Writers Retreat at Hawthornden Castle in Scotland. He is the Philippine editor for *MANOA: A Pacific Journal of International Writing,* published by the University of Hawaii. A founding member of the Philippine Literary Arts Council, Manila Critics Circle, and Creative Writing Foundation, Inc., he currently chairs the Writers Union of the Philippines. He teaches Fiction and Poetry at the Ateneo de Manila University and writes a regular arts & culture column for a national daily, *The Philippine Star.*